HARLEY QUINN™
at SUPER HERO HIGH

HARLEY QUINN™
at SUPER HERO HIGH

By Lisa Yee

Random House 🏠 New York

For Rob, who makes me laugh

All rights reserved. Published in the United States by Random House Children's
Books, a division of Penguin Random House LLC, New York, and in Canada by
Penguin Random House Canada Limited, Toronto. Random House and the colophon
are registered trademarks of Penguin Random House LLC.
Visit us on the Web!
rhcbooks.com
dcsuperherogirls.com
dckids.com
ISBN 978-1-5247-6923-9 (hc)—ISBN 978-1-5247-6924-6 (lib. bdg.)—
ISBN 978-1-5247-6925-3 (ebook)
Printed in the United States of America
10 9 8 7 6 5 4 3 2 1

PROLOGUE

That the teenaged sword-wielding hero Katana had just been named Super Hero of the Month was no surprise. After all, she had solved the mystery surrounding the death of her grandmother, Onna-bugeisha Yamashiro—the first female super hero samurai. Plus, she had set things right for the mysterious Ghost Crabs that had invaded Super Hero High *and* saved the world from the evil villain Dragon King and his army of mutated reptilian warriors.

So what did all that mean for the students at Super Hero High?

It was time for cake!

There was always a celebration when Super Hero of the Month was announced, and Bumblebee had planned a little surprise for Katana.

"How did you know it would be me?" Katana asked. Her straight black hair glistened and her big brown eyes were bright. There was a rosy flush to her pale complexion from all the attention.

Other students, like the irrepressible jokester Harley

Quinn, loved being in the spotlight, and even sought it out. But not Katana. To her it was just something to get used to, like fighting interplanetary villains or getting her homework in on time.

"Oh, I had a hunch," a tiny voice said from beneath the lemon butter cake that was flying across the room. The cake boasted a citrus sugar glaze and the words *Congrats, Katana!* written in royal red icing.

From underneath the cake, Bumblebee grew from bee-sized to girl-sized as she set it down. Thick honey-colored streaks accentuated her rich brown curly hair, and even though her yellow insect wings may have looked delicate, they were anything but. Having delivered the cake, she treated herself to a small taste of the icing with her finger. She looked around the room as the party took shape.

Supergirl had snuck in and decorated Katana's dorm room with colorful balloons and streamers, and Poison Ivy had filled it with Katana's favorite Japanese snowball flowers.

"Achoo! Achooo! Achooooo!"

Near Katana's display of swords someone was sneezing loudly. "Achooooosie woozie!" the girl in the blue shorts and mismatched tights said with gusto.

"Is the word *subtle* in her vocabulary?" Cheetah asked as she waited impatiently for the cake to be cut.

"Isn't anyone going to say gesundheit?" the girl in the blue shorts asked.

"Gesundheit," said several voices around the room.

The black mask over her eyes could not hide her look of mischief. "**YOWZERS!** Those are some mighty flowers," she continued. "They're killing my allergies. Killing 'em, I tell you." The girl was Harley Quinn. She might have seemed unfocused, but she was looking at one person in particular.

"Hey, over here! Katana, am I going to score this interview or am I going to score this interview?" Harley quipped. She somersaulted through the partygoers. Her blond pigtails, streaked with red and blue, kept bouncing even when she stood still.

"I need to do this first," Katana said. She picked up the cake and threw it. Before it smashed into the ceiling, Katana unsheathed her sword, leapt, and in midair, expertly cut it into three dozen pieces. Each identically sized slice landed on one of the plates lined up in rows on the table.

"I love cake!" Big Barda announced as she took the first piece. She removed her heavy gold-and-black helmet and set it aside. Cake was serious business.

Harley gave Katana a big impatient smile. The young samurai knew that there was no stopping Harley when she wanted something. And right now Harley wanted one of her famous "exclusively exclusive Harley Quinn's Harley's Quinntessentials scoops"!

"Your fave hostess with the mostest, Harley Quinn, here," the Web star said, beaming into the camera.

Harley took a large bite of cake, leaving some frosting on her nose. When Katana pointed this out, Harley thanked her, added more frosting, and waggled her eyebrows at her digital audience.

"Just clowning around," she told her viewers. "But this is serious stuff now. Seriously awesome! I've got Katana in person to tell us how she felt when she heard she was Super Hero High's Super Hero of the Month."

Katana blinked into the camera. Not everyone was as comfortable as Harley was at being broadcast to thousands of viewers. Harley's Web channel had been a hit since its debut. There was no telling how many viewers she could get.

"It feels pretty great," Katana said. "But it was a team effort—"

"Aww, she's too modest!" Harley interrupted, turning the camera on herself and reenacting Katana's martial arts moves. "Boom! Boom! Blam! Blam! Slice and dice! You shoulda seen this girl wielding her sword. It was like she was holding a bolt of lightning! Speaking of lightning, let's chat with everyone's fav-o-rite weather-themed super hero sisters, Thunder and Lightning."

Before Thunder could answer, Harley dashed off into the crowd. Thunder stood confused, and tugged on the V-neck collar of her sleek black-and-electric-yellow costume. The yellow barrettes that held her bangs in place matched her boots. Her sister, Lightning, crouched down to tie her high-top sneakers. Her sporty clothes made her look like she was always ready for action.

"That was weird," Lightning said. "Harley was just talking to us and now she's gone . . . again."

"*She's* weird," Thunder said, quickly adding, "But I mean that in the best way!"

Just then, everyone heard a familiar voice. Only it didn't sound normal.

"Help!" Harley was crying. "Someone help me!"

CHAPTER 1

"Harley's such a crack-up," Cheetah said, rolling her eyes. "Class clowns are like that." Supergirl, hovering nearby, was carrying all the empty plates in two five-foot stacks. She frowned at her feline classmate.

"We should check this out," Wonder Woman announced, always attuned to possible trouble. She tossed her plate so it landed on Supergirl's stack, then adjusted the golden cuffs on her wrists. She motioned the others to follow her as she tracked the sound of Harley's voice.

"Help!"

Everyone could hear Harley still yelling. But as they turned the corner, Harley was nowhere to be seen. Instead, her ever-present video camera was on the floor.

Bumblebee ran to pick it up. She looked at the video screen. On it was Harley yelling "Help! Someone help me!" Then the screen went dark.

"This doesn't look good," Bumblebee said.

Batgirl watched over Bumblebee's shoulder as Bumblebee

replayed the video. "Harley's in trouble!" Batgirl said. "She would never be without her camera."

Wonder Woman looked perplexed. "I don't see anything," she said, staring at the blackness on the screen.

"Exactly," said Batgirl. "But when I hit 'Playback,' you can hear her. Listen."

Sure enough, it was the first sound of Harley crying for help that they had all heard.

Instantly, the Supers snapped into action.

"I'll check the school . . . ," The Flash said, racing away at super-speed before he had even finished his sentence.

"I'll search the underground caverns," Katana volunteered.

"I'll inform Principal Waller," Hawkgirl announced.

"Wait!" Batgirl called out.

Those who remained crammed around the small video screen. They gasped when Harley's face appeared. She was laughing. "Gotcha!" Harley said. "I'm okay, it was all just a joke! I'm fine. I . . ."

Just then, a menacing shadow came up behind her, and suddenly the screen went dark and silent.

As Supers fanned out over the school and across Metropolis to save their friend, Harley wasn't far from where she had disappeared. The truth was, she wasn't even in danger.

Instead, Harley was laughing from the top of the school's iconic Crystal Tower.

"This is gonna make great entertainment!" Harley said. She had a habit of talking to herself. That way, it always seemed like someone was with her. Having planned ahead, Harley had placed remote cameras around campus. "Everyone's going to tune in!" she told herself. "And then when I reveal my hiding—"

"You are in so much trouble!" a familiar voice growled. Harley looked up, surprised to find Cheetah glaring down at her with her hands on her hips. Cheetah's long brown hair whipped behind her.

"Harley, you forgot I have super-vision," Supergirl said, landing from above and making sure not to step on Cheetah's tail with her red high-top sneakers. "I spotted you as soon as I flew above campus and looked back."

Supergirl yelled down to Beast Boy, who was slithering around in the form of a green snake, checking out low, hard-to-get-to areas. "Alert the Supers on the ground that Harley has been found and she's safe! I'll tell the ones in the sky," she said, leaping off the tower and flying away.

Beast Boy turned back into his scruffy green teen self for a moment before changing into a small coqui frog. Despite his now-minuscule size, his voice could generate sounds as high as one hundred decibels—as loud as a jackhammer.

He croaked, "Harley Quinn has been found. Harley Quinn is safe. Harley Quinn has been found. Harley Quinn is safe. Harley Quinn has been found. . . ."

Except for her light blue eyes narrowing with disapproval, Cheetah hadn't moved.

"What?" Harley asked, feigning innocence. "Would you like to say a few words to our Harley's Quinntessentials viewers?"

"Put the camera down," Cheetah said. "Everyone's looking for you. They think you're in danger."

"I was," Harley said, laughing. She loved to laugh. She laughed at everything really. "I was in danger of not having enough viewers. But now, everyone will tune in to my new 'Find Harley' segment! I was secretly videoing your reactions, and they were priceless. Score one for Harley!"

"Score zero," Cheetah said. "I'm going to tell Principal Waller that it was all just a joke from our resident class clown. Then we'll see who's laughing."

"No one is laughing," Principal Waller was saying, her back to Harley Quinn. Harley could see in the reflection in the office window that the principal's normally stern face looked even more serious. Harley didn't even think that was possible. The Wall, as Principal Amanda Waller was often called—though never to her face—had a look that would make Ares, the god of war and Wonder Woman's half-brother, cry.

Harley squirmed on the wooden chair across from Waller's desk. "Put the ice blaster back," the principal ordered, without looking. "I've asked you before not to touch things on my desk."

"Yes, Principal Waller," Harley said, quickly placing it back on top of the pile of confiscated weapons.

All weapons were supposed to be checked in and assigned tracking numbers, but students were always forgetting this formality. Well-meaning parents sent swords, chemicals, lasers, and other items that they thought their kids might find useful at school. And some students, like Poison Ivy and Cyborg, were always coming up with new ways to weaponize everyday objects for Lucius Fox's Weaponomics class. That was fine for class, but it wasn't something Waller could allow in the common areas.

"That little stunt you pulled, about going missing. What do you have to say for yourself?" Principal Waller demanded.

"It was just for giggles . . . and a twenty-three percent increase in viewership," Harley answered innocently. "And math! I'm using what I learned in class and applying it to my channel." She aimed her infectious grin at the principal. When Waller didn't respond, Harley ramped up her smile.

After years heading up Super Hero High, the principal was immune to the charms of her students, even ones as lovable as Harley Quinn.

"I see," said Waller. "How about this, then: zero new Harley's Quinntessentials videos plus detention. For two weeks." The Wall's eyes stayed locked with Harley's as she smiled warmly and added, "Math."

CHAPTER 2

That afternoon in the dining hall, no one would look at Harley. "What did I do?" she implored. "What did I do?"

"If you don't know, then maybe you should think about it," Wonder Woman said to be helpful.

Harley set her tray down between Katana and Bumblebee. Both scooted over to give her room—more room than usual.

"What did I do?" she asked as Star Sapphire strolled past, giving her a chilly look.

"Think about it," Wonder Woman reminded Harley.

"Psst," Harley whispered to Bumblebee. "Give me a hint."

Bumblebee was busy pouring honey over her spaghetti. She really liked honey. On everything.

"Harley," Katana said. "People are mad at you for making them think you were in danger. That's not funny."

"*You* were worried," Harley said, slumping in her chair so her head barely appeared above the table. "*I'm* worried! Waller banned any new Harley's Quinntessentials videos for two weeks! I'm in reruns. For seven days times two! She even confiscated my video cameras. I won't have any viewers left when I return with fresh stuff."

Katana frowned. "Is that what you're worried about?" she said. "How many viewers you have?"

"Well, yes!" Harley said. "You got that right!"

Katana let go of a heavy sigh. "There's more to life than viewers," she said.

Harley topped her mountain of garlic mashed potatoes with a cherry. "Not if you're Harley Quinn," she declared.

"Hiya, fellow detainees!" Harley said as she cartwheeled into the after-school detention room. She waved to Frost and Lady Shiva. Both looked bored.

"Everyone take a seat, and no talking!" Vice Principal Grodd grumbled. His red bow tie matched the hankie in his suit coat pocket. Grodd was very dapper for a gorilla.

Harley let out an audible sigh and sat next to Poison Ivy. The flowers in her long red hair were wilting.

"Whatcha in for?" Harley asked brightly. She wasn't about to let anyone know she was bummed. Even though Harley could make almost anything fun, there were dozens of places she'd rather be than detention.

Poison Ivy shook her head. "Chompy got out of hand

again," she said.

Harley nodded. Everyone knew Ivy's large and overactive pet plant. Whenever Chompy overgrew his latest pot and went wild, it took Parasite, the janitor, a full day to clean up the mess.

On Harley's other side, The Flash was leaning so far back in his chair that three of its legs were off the ground. Harley passed him a note. It read,

What are you in for?

He waited until Grodd was fully engrossed in his *101 Banana Recipes* book.

The Flash wrote back.

Breaking the sound barrier—twice. Sounds awesome!

Harley wrote in her loopy scrawl. She drew a sad face.

Poison Ivy cleared her throat. She pointed to Grodd, who had fallen asleep and was now snoring gruffly. "Don't wake him," she whispered. "We have to stay out of trouble!"

Harley attempted to look serious, but failed. "Me, stay out of trouble?" she said. "Not possible!"

Without Harley's Quinntessentials to keep her busy, Harley had a lot of free time—not when she was in detention, of course, but all the hours she normally spent on her Web

channel were now open.

"Two weeks! She might as well have said forever!" Harley said, moaning in her booth at the Capes & Cowls Café.

"One extra-large sweet potato fries with four sides of ketchup!" Steve Trevor announced, placing the order in front of her. He had just gotten a trim, and now his blond hair was a tad too short. "Hey, Harley, with your channel in reruns, I don't know what's happening at Super Hero High. Um . . . how's Wonder Woman?" He blushed. "I'm asking for a friend."

Steve's dad owned Capes & Cowls Café, and though he wasn't a super hero, Steve worked as hard as one. The restaurant was a mishmash of homey and trendy that the Super Hero High students loved.

Regular teens and Supers alike—and even some of the teachers—went there. Steve always set aside a dozen apple cider doughnuts for Batgirl's father, Police Commissioner Gordon.

Harley picked up a sweet potato fry and pointed it toward the door. "There's Wonder Woman," she said. "Let's ask her!"

Before Steve could stop her, Harley shouted, "Hey, Wonder Woman! Wonder Woman, over here!" Harley waved, then pointed to Steve, who looked like he was trying to make himself invisible. "Stevie here has been asking about you! Come talk to him!"

Wonder Woman blushed as red as the star on her gold

tiara. The only person who was a brighter red was Steve . . . and Red Tornado, the school's flight teacher, who had stopped in for a strawberry smoothie. But then, he was always that red.

"When is your channel going to be back up?" Star Sapphire asked Harley from the next table. She played with the power ring on her finger.

Harley could only stare at the purple glow coming from the ring. "Pretty!" she said, her attention shifted away from Wonder Woman and Steve.

"I have a scoop for you," Sapphire whispered. Frost, who was sitting next to her, raised her eyebrow inquiringly as she blew on her peppermint tea, turning it ice-cold.

"Whatcha got?" Harley asked, snapping to attention. A scoop! Harley loved nothing more than getting news first. Her motto was *All the news, as it happens . . . and sometimes even before!*

"I heard from a little bird that we're finally getting a new music teacher," Sapphire said.

"It's about time!" Harley whistled with approval. "Can't wait to interview her. Or him. Do you know who it'll be?"

Sapphire smoothed the front of her pink and purple dress. The insignia on her belt matched the one on her jeweled headband, which matched the color of her ring.

Harley took note of her own clothes: a black, white, and red checkered shirt with short black sleeves, and blue jean shorts with a thin belt over colored tights—black on one side, red on the other. All with comfortable chunky blue sneakers on her feet. Harley felt a little sad . . . for Star Sapphire. *If only everyone could have a costume as fun, fashionable, and functional as min*e, she thought.

"I hear it's a he, and he's starting soon," said Sapphire, reminding Harley of what they were talking about. "By the way, you will be featuring me on Harley's Quinntessentials when you're back on the air, right?"

"You betcha!" Harley assured her. Fashionistas always tuned in when Star Sapphire was on her show.

As Harley settled back to contemplate her happy return to the Internet, she noticed a familiar figure at the counter. She grabbed her plate and plopped down next to her. "Heya, Lois! What's the new news?"

Lois Lane pushed her glasses up and smiled. "Hi, Harley. I heard about Harley's Quinntessentials going on hiatus."

"Yeah, well, Waller's trying to teach me a lesson," Harley said nonchalantly—with a shrug that said, "In the meantime, I guess that means you'll get all the scoops!"

"We're not in competition," Lois said. "I report the news, and you do news and entertainment."

Harley glanced at the jukebox. Captain Cold from CAD Academy had it blasting a retro rock song. The music inspired Beast Boy to lead a bunch of kids in a dance in the middle of the café.

"Well, just news is boring," Harley mused as a conga line of teens weaved in and out of the café. "Booor-ring! Oopsie, sorry—you know what I mean," she said to the teen reporter.

"No need to apologize. It can be boring," Lois said, laughing. "But straight-up news is what I'm interested in. What are you interested in?"

Harley tugged on a pigtail, watching it bounce when she let go. "I'm interested in having the most viewers in Metropolis. No, wait—in the world and beyond!"

"You've always thought big," said Lois. "Harley, you're a force to be reckoned with. Half of your audience tunes in to see the inside story on the Supers—and you have all prime access to that—and the other half tunes in to see you!"

"Little ol' me?" Harley said with a twinkle in her eye. She did a backflip onto a table. "Why would anyone want to look at me?" Harley said, her arms raised dramatically above her head as kids in the café applauded.

"Um. Harley," Steve said, wiping his hand on a towel. "Remember, we talked about no standing on tables."

Harley giggled. "Right-O, Steve-O," she said. "My bad."

CHAPTER 3

After Lois left, Harley continued to peck at her fries, but she couldn't stop thinking about what the young reporter had said. She wondered what might happen if she did more than cover the falls, foibles, and fantastic happenings of her fellow Supers, like Star Sapphire's Fashion Fix It. What if she did specials like . . .

It was hard to concentrate. Steve had recently installed the retro jukebox. It was all bright lights and neon colors, and music, music, music. It seemed like half the restaurant was dancing to the music. Most of the kids were just goofing off, but a few were really talented.

As she watched, Harley's brain began to go into overdrive. She had so many ideas it was hard for her to keep up with herself. Finally, one thought hit Harley so hard that she yelled, "OUCH!"

She jumped up and dashed out the door.

"Hey, Lois!" Harley called, running after her. By then Lois

was in Centennial Park. "Slow down! I have something to ask you."

Lois looked curious. "Yes?"

"Okay, okay. News, yes. News is news. But when it's not new anymore, it's not news, right?" Harley reasoned.

"I . . . think so?" Lois said slowly. "What are you saying, Harley?"

"I'm saying, what if I expanded Harley's Quinntessentials beyond Super Hero High? What if I took the news and turned it into entertainment?" Harley looked right at Lois. "What if I broadcast a dance contest? And what if it was live so everyone everywhere could tune in? That way we'd all know the winner at the same time! I'd be making the news instead of just reporting it! Isn't that a great idea? A totally **WOWZA-YOWZA** of an idea! I'll have more viewers than I'll know what to do with! I'll have so many viewers that—"

"Whoa, whoa, slow down," Lois said. She waited patiently for Harley to stop with the somersaults. "You do know that there's a difference between informing your viewers with the news and entertaining, right?"

When Harley gave her a blank stare, Lois tried again. "The news is fact. We strive to tell our viewers the truth and inform them about what's happening in the world. Especially when the information may impact them."

"Yes!" Harley agreed "Impact them! That's what I plan to do. POW! I'm going to have reality shows on Harley's

Quinntessentials! And the first show will be a dance competition called Harley's Dance-O-Rama! What do you think of that?"

Lois gave Harley a weak smile. "Um, okay," she said. "But it sounds more like entertainment than—"

"It sounds like blockbuster ratings, that's what it sounds like!" Harley assured her.

There were only two more days left in detention. Vice Principal Grodd had finished his banana recipe book and was now reading a cookbook called *Bamboo and You*. As he sat munching on a stalk, the Supers shifted in their seats. Blessed with powers like super-speed, super-strength, and enhanced mental abilities, they weren't good at staying still.

In the back corner, Poison Ivy kept sticking her head into her backpack and talking. When she saw Harley staring at her, she offered a sheepish grin. "I'm comforting one of my baby daffodils," Ivy whispered apologetically. "She's lonely." A petite yellow flower peered out from the backpack and then quickly retreated. Harley smiled. Poison Ivy was crazy about her plants, and they were crazy about her, too.

Outside the window, Supergirl was zooming in and out of the clouds, playing bow-and-arrow boomerang. In the game, Arrowette, whose family's archery skills were legendary, would take her stance, draw her bow, aim into the sky, and release an arrow. As the arrow hurtled at almost four hundred feet per second, Supergirl would catch it and then throw it back. Their record was fifteen in fifteen seconds.

Harley opened her notebook. There was a big HQ in blue and red on the cover. Inside, in her loopy handwriting, were her notes for the Dance-O-Rama. It was all coming together—on paper, at least. Once her Web channel was back up and running, the real fun could start. But first Harley needed some help.

That night Harley stood at the front of the room and said, "You're all probably wondering why I asked you here."

Beast Boy had a giant red-pepper pizza in front of him. "I thought we were in the dining hall for dinner," he said, folding the pizza in half and eating it like a taco.

"I want to know why we're here," Big Barda said. She had so many servings of mashed potatoes on her plate, it looked like the Swiss Alps had relocated.

As Harley told the Supers about her Dance-O-Rama, some ignored her, but others seemed interested. Hawkgirl raised her hand. "So let me get this straight. Heroes and villains will be allowed to try out to be contestants?"

"That's right!" Harley said. "And regular citizens, too. It's open to all."

"And you can have as many people on your team as you want?" Supergirl asked.

"And as few," Hawkgirl added. She had been taking notes. "You can be a soloist."

"I can be a soloist?" Wonder Woman asked.

"Anyone can," said Harley.

"What are the rules?" asked Hawkgirl.

"Who needs rules?" said Harley.

"The contest does," Hawkgirl said. "Otherwise it will be chaos."

"Would chaos be so bad?" Harley asked.

"It could be," Supergirl said. "Have you run this past Principal Waller yet?"

Harley suddenly got serious. **YOWZA!** If anyone could stand in the way of this great idea, it would be the Wall.

"Let me understand this, Ms. Quinn," Principal Waller said. Already an imposing figure, she was wearing one of her severe dark gray suits. Waller had seven of them, one for every day of the week.

Bumblebee flew into and out of the office, delivering

papers and passing along messages. When Bumblebee saw Harley, she offered her a warm smile. Harley smiled back. She appreciated Bumblebee's upbeat nature. *Too many Supers are stressed out and so serious*, Harley lamented as a dozen other thoughts bounced around in her head.

"Dancing?" Waller continued, making it sound like Harley had asked permission to hold a worm-eating contest. "And you want to enlist some of my students to help you? And you want open auditions—ones in which a contestant's past is not of consequence? And you want to broadcast the contest live from Super Hero High on your Web channel?"

Harley gulped. When Waller said it, hosting a Dance-O-Rama didn't sound so fun.

"Yes, ma'am," Harley mumbled.

"Well, Harley." Waller shuffled some papers on her desk. "I think it's a great idea."

Harley got up and made her way to the door. "Yeah, yeah, got it. I hear ya, I hear ya. No dance contest. Anyway, thanks for listening."

CHAPTER 4

As Harley dragged herself down the hall, the sound of buzzing got louder.

"Harley, wait. Waller sent me to talk to you," Bumblebee called after her.

Harley stopped to pull up her socks. They were always falling. "Am I in trouble again?" she asked. Despite her best efforts, it seemed like Harley was always getting called out. Most people, she decided, did not have her refined sense of humor and penchant for fun. Harley held up her hands. "**YOWZA.** I surrender already. Arrest me!" she joked.

Bumblebee's laugh was light and warm, like honey. "There's no need for that," she assured her. "Waller thinks you didn't understand. Harley, she was giving you permission to go ahead and hold the dance contest!"

"Wha-wha-what?" Harley blabbered. Her jumbled thoughts were spinning.

When Bumblebee nodded, Harley's whoop of joy could

be heard all the way to the athletic field. "Yes!" she yelled. "Get ready, world! Harley's Dance-O-Rama is going to be the biggest and best-est dance contest anyone has ever seen. Ratings are gonna go straight through the roof, pierce the clouds, and ricochet off the stars!"

Big Barda was tossing huge weights to Supergirl, who tossed them to Wonder Woman, who was stacking them up so the Supers would have something to knock down.

"Does this look crooked?" Wonder Woman asked as she stepped back to appraise the pile.

Across the room, Miss Martian was nervously dangling several feet above the floor from a rope that was part of a training exercise.

"And . . . go!" Coach Wildcat yelled as he lit the bottom of the frayed rope with a match. It looked like an upside-down Fourth of July sparkler. "Miss Martian, you'd better start climbing the rope before the fire catches up to you!"

Frost stood by the sidelines and tried not to yawn. She was there to put out the fire if needed.

As the rope began to sizzle, Miss Martian scampered up. Her brown eyes were big with misgiving, and her long red hair covered her face. She had never gone so high or so fast before! Poison Ivy stood by and applauded.

"Good!" Wildcat barked. "El Diablo, you're up next! Replace that rope and then climb it, stat!"

In another part of the gym, Katana was twirling swords so fast you could hear them slicing the air. Cyborg tried to do the same. However, the sound he made was the metal clang when he accidentally hit himself with the weapon time and time again. "Pick it up and try again," Katana encouraged him. "And don't worry about dents. You can get those fixed later."

"'Scuse me, Coach Wildcat," Harley said, tapping him on the shoulder. It was as solid as cement. "May I have a few minutes of your time?"

Wildcat turned around, his face in a scowl. "Is this important?" he asked. "I have super heroes to train."

"It's super-duper important, Coach!" Harley assured him.

"You really think teaching dance during PE is a good idea?" Wildcat asked as El Diablo accidentally lit the bleachers on fire. Frost put out the flames by sending a blast of ice over them. Wildcat jerked his head around as a blur burst past. "Hey, Flash, speed it up!" he yelled.

Wildcat looked serious as he turned back to Harley, who nodded eagerly.

Geez. There's so much seriousness around school, Harley

thought in the face of Wildcat's unending scowl. *Good thing they have me.*

"This is a physical education class," the coach reminded her. "These Supers need to be agile and alert at all times. After all, they may be saving the world someday, and that someday could be sooner than anyone thinks. Harley," he said, "give me three good reasons why I should even be listening to you talk about dancing."

Harley had anticipated this. She turned to Batgirl and nodded. Clinging to the ceiling using one of her B.A.T. (Barbara-Assisted Technology) devices, Batgirl hit "On" and Harley's POWer (Project, Out-logic, and Wow) presentation appeared on the east wall.

"One," Harley began as a photo of exuberant octogenarians dancing appeared, "dancing makes for strong bones. Two, it helps increase stamina. Three, it improves memory by making us recall steps and routines. Four, balance is called into play, strengthening our core muscles. Five—"

"Enough!" Wildcat said, raising his paw. "Enough already, Harley!"

She paused and held her breath.

"I'll give you gym periods three and four. But if I don't see results and it's a bust," Coach Wildcat warned, "then you'll be mopping the floors alongside Parasite until Doomsday. Got it?"

"Got it, Mr. Coach Wildcat, sir," she promised. "Harley Quinn won't let you down!"

The next day, Harley's classes seemed *sooo looong*. She just couldn't sit still. In Crazy Quilt's Super Suits design class, Harley kept applauding and whistling, hoping to speed things up.

"Harley, Harley, Harley!" Crazy Quilt said as he sauntered down the catwalk that split the room in half. "Please hold your applause until the situation merits it." He stopped mid-runway and stuck a disco pose. When the class was silent, Crazy Quilt whispered to Harley, "You can applaud now."

At last! The class she was waiting for. Harley was bouncing off the walls. Literally.

"Quiet!" Wildcat blew his whistle and then waited for the Supers to be silent. These were the elite teens of the universe, the super heroes of tomorrow . . . but for now, they were typical energetic teenagers in PE class.

"CALM DOWN!" Harley yelled. "This is important." She looked at Wildcat and said reassuringly, "Go ahead, Coach."

Wildcat scowled and continued. "Yesterday we learned how to disable our detractors with head locks, hard punches, and elbows to the solar plexus. Today we're going to learn pivots, pirouettes, and a do-si-do or two, thanks to Harley Quinn's suggestion. That's right: we're all going to dance! And anyone who thinks they can't learn a thing or two from me about cha-cha-cha-ing is in for a surprise."

Hawkgirl frowned. Beast Boy grinned. Harley did an aerial, and when she nailed her landing she pointed to Wildcat and announced, "Supers, you're looking at the Ranger Ridge State College dance champion! Give it up for Coach 'Crazy Legs' Wildcat!"

"That's ancient history," he said with a modest grin. "But think about it. The best battles are like choreographed dance routines. It's a give and take, and there's a rhythm to it."

"How about heating up this class with a little salsa dancing?" said El Diablo.

"How about a little polka?" Wildcat asked.

"How about a little *polka* in the eye," Harley whispered to Bumblebee, then laughed at her own joke.

"Polka?" El Diablo said. The black images of flames that adorned his arms rippled. "That's so old-school."

Parasite, the school janitor, was sweeping up under the bleachers. "Polka's not old-school," Harley heard him grumble. "The easier it looks, the harder it is."

"Okay," Wildcat called out. "Pick your partners."

"You heard him," Harley yelled. She began clapping. "Let's go! Let's go! Let's go!"

Wildcat looked at her sideways. Harley shrugged. "I figured you need a dance assistant, and that person ought to be me."

There was a mad rush. Big Barda and Supergirl stood together. Green Lantern and Lady Shiva were happily chatting. Cheetah and Star Sapphire were conspiring. Everyone had a partner except one student, who stood on the sidelines.

"Miss Martian," Wildcat said. "I'm sorry, but there's an odd number of dancers, so I'm afraid you'll just have to sit this one out."

"That's fine," Miss Martian said softly. She began to fade until no one could see her.

"Dancers," Wildcat bellowed. "I want you to watch this video first, and then we polka!"

At a school full of super heroes, everyone wanted to be the best, whether at battling intergalactic villains, outsmarting criminals, or doing a polka. They studied the video of big-skirted women and men in jaunty vests with a keen interest. Hawkgirl took notes. Bumblebee danced in place.

"Okay, ready?" Wildcat asked. He didn't wait for an answer. "And . . . go!"

CHAPTER 5

As the relentlessly upbeat strains of accordion and clarinet pumped through the gym, an imposing figure stepped into the room. Amanda Waller's face was unreadable as she watched her students galloping and gallumphing in pairs.

"Big step, small step! Small step!" Wildcat was calling as he clapped his paws to the beat. "That's right! Big step, half step, half step. Full, half, half . . . No, no, Wonder Woman and Supergirl, no flying. This is on the ground only. Flash, slow down. Barda, Katana, it's not all big steps!"

"You heard him!" Harley called out, bouncing up and down to the music. "Big step, small step!"

The Supers were bumping into each other, causing some to crash against the walls and/or knock over the other dancers. They were all enjoying the confusion, especially Harley—until she noticed Principal Waller staring at something at the far end of the gym.

"**WOWZA!**" Harley said, pointing. "Do you see what I see?"

Soon everyone was watching Parasite doing an incredible polka . . . alone. His eyes were closed as he deftly moved through the steps, lost in the music.

There was a collective gasp as his partner slowly appeared. Miss Martian was smiling as she polkaed around the gym with the janitor. As they continued to skip and spin, Waller nodded to Wildcat before leaving.

When the music ended, the applause began. Parasite was a little out of breath. It took great control to dance and keep his powers in check—he had the ability to drain Supers of their powers. But Miss Martian was beaming. "Thank you," she said bashfully.

"Thank *you*," he said, giving her a small bow before he picked up his broom. He tried not to smile amid the calls of "Great job!" and "Parasite, you're the polka king!"

Wildcat looked at Miss Martian. "Next time," he said, "you will show these Supers how it's done."

"How would you describe yourself?" Bumblebee asked the girls who were crowded around her locker. She was holding the "What Super Are You?" quiz in *Super Student, Super Star* magazine.

Harley didn't hesitate. "I'm the frosting on the cake! The *zzazz* in *pizzazz*! The ribbon on the present! The duper in super!" she said, leaping up and then taking a bow.

Cheetah strolled past and commented, "What you are is a class clown."

Frost followed, laughing. "Where's your red nose?" she asked.

Harley lit up. "Thanks for the reminder!" She pulled a red foam nose seemingly from out of nowhere and plopped it on her nose. Then Harley grabbed her book bag and headed to class, leaving a trail of giggles, guffaws, and shocked expressions in her wake as she made her way down the hall yelling, "Clown comin' through!"

The line into the gym snaked out of the building and wrapped around the base of Crystal Tower. Twice.

"Lookit!" Harley cried. "Look at the semifinalists! We're gonna have big fun!"

Just a few days earlier, Harley's Quinntessentials had gone back on the air with new segments. "Hey, Harley fans," she had broadcast. "Didja miss me? I sure missed you, and you're not gonna wanna miss this—Harley's Dance-O-Rama!"

The buzz for the Dance-O-Rama was so big that even Lois Lane reported on it. "Word is that dancers from around the world and beyond are eager to show their moves," Lois had said.

"I'm glad I had everyone check in online before they showed up," Batgirl told Beast Boy as she consulted the mini-computer on her wrist. "Each entry was given a number. We have one hundred eighty-seven dance groups and thirty-seven soloists for the semifinals. Good thing we had the groups send in tapes for us to cull through first. Otherwise we'd have more contestants than people in the entire city of Metropolis!"

"Thirty-eight soloists," Beast Boy corrected her.

"No, thirty-seven," Batgirl said, triple-checking the list.

"A super-talented last-minute performer just showed up," Beast Boy told her. He began to moonwalk. "We don't want to leave this one out. This will rock the ratings, believe me!"

Harley's eyes grew big. "Who is it?" she asked, scanning the crowd.

"Me!" Beast Boy said, stopping and pointing to himself. "Right here. Right now. With all the right moves."

Batgirl shook her head. "You were supposed to send in an audition tape like everyone else."

Beast Boy turned into a dancing hippo and gracefully balanced on one foot. "But I'm not like everyone else," he noted. "I'm special."

Bumblebee flew up. As official troubleshooter, it was her job to take care of any unforeseen problems. "There's no time for arguing, people," she reminded everyone.

"Then it's settled! Let's let him in," Harley proclaimed, adding, "He'll be good for ratings!"

It was an odd gathering as the contestants descended on Super Hero High. A whole contingent from the Planet XOXO were dressed as puffy Valentine hearts, a trio of break-dancers from CAD Academy had brought a crate of plates and coffee cups with them, and what looked like half of Korugar Academy was present. Plus, there were dance teams from almost every regular high school, villains who had come out of hiding to show off their samba skills, and even one hundred tap dancers from Tap Dance Town, that new senior citizen community for retired super hero sidekicks.

It was sure to be a spectacle, and Harley had placed cameras around the gym to capture every dance move.

"Three, two, one . . . and we're live!" Harley turned to the camera as two Furies from Apokolips Magnet stormed the stage looking confident.

Big Barda fiddled with the sound system, making sure it was working. Barda took her job as DJ seriously, and her status as a Super Hero High student even more seriously. Normally, Bumblebee would have DJ'ed, but as the show's troubleshooter, she was already swamped.

"Welcome to Harley's Quinntessentials," Harley said gleefully, "or HQ, to my friends. Today we usher in a new show. Yes! It's time for the semifinals of our **POW! BANG! WHAM! WOWZA!** of a spectacle, the Harley's Dance-O-Rama! And now let's get started! First up, the Furies!"

The duo from the dark and desolate planet started off slowly, but with each powerful stomp, their hip-hop dance ramped up until the entire school was shaking. When the music stopped, Furies Stompa and Lashina looked triumphantly at the DJ standing behind the music console.

"Hey, Barda, see what you're missing?" Lashina snarled, tossing her black-and-blue ponytail over her shoulder.

Stompa took a bow. "You should never have left Apokolips," she said when they walked past their former schoolmate. Her heavy boots made the gym tremble beneath Big Barda's feet.

"It's okay, Barda," Supergirl said, quickly flying over. "You're one of us now. Those bad days at Apokolips are—"

Harley interrupted. "C'mon, c'mon, we got a show to put on!" she reminded them with a circular motion of her arm that said "Let's keep the ball rolling."

Hawkgirl consulted her watch. Harley had named her stage manager, and as with all her assignments, she wanted to make sure everything was perfect.

"Katana, we're ready for the next group," Hawkgirl said into her headset. "Send in the clowns."

CHAPTER 6

Howls of laugher rippled through the stands as the clowns pushed and pulled and tumbled over each other to get to the stage.

"Wait for me!" Harley cried, joining them.

"Oh, look! It's our very own class clown, doing her thing," Cheetah said as Harley rolled past her.

"It's going to be just as hard to corral Harley as the contestants!" Batgirl shouted to Big Barda, who cued up the circus music.

The Comic Conga Clowns soon had everyone in the stands dancing in one long line around the gym and out the building. When the first clown in front leaned back, so did everyone else. And when she sat down, it caused a chain reaction of everyone falling into the lap of the person behind them.

Harley could not stop laughing, nor could anyone watching. Though the semifinals had just begun, she was having a great time, and the dancers kept coming: samba, tango, foxtrot. Polka. Belly dancing. Ballet. Every kind of dance imaginable was being demonstrated.

"And now, another group from my own Super Hero High!" Harley said into the camera. "Here are Green Lantern, Raven, Catwoman, and Starfire doing their rendition of swing dancing!"

Batgirl was monitoring the online viewership. There were hundreds of thousands of viewers from every corner of the universe. She even detected some views from another galaxy. The show was breaking records. Batgirl had to admit: Harley knew how to entertain a crowd.

"And that's all for today!" Harley announced. "Tomorrow, we will resume our semifinals! So, until then, keep watching and keep laughing," she said as her channel started replaying the day's events.

If Harley Quinn had her way, Harley's Quinntessentials would be live 24/7. But Waller had put limitations on how much time she could broadcast. There was, after all, something called "school."

"That was exhausting," Batgirl said as they crowded into Harley's dorm.

"Everyone, thank you for all your help in making the

Dance-O-Rama a hit!" Harley enthused. "Just wait until tomorrow, when we name the finalists. That's gonna be big!"

"I'll bet you're going to get zillions of messages telling you how great you are," Miss Martian noted, looking at Harley with admiration. "I wonder what that's like?"

"What what's like?" asked Harley.

"To be you," said Miss Martian. "To have so many fans, and to get fan mail."

"It's the best!" Harley exclaimed. "Fans make you feel good, and fan mail can make you feel even better."

This Harley knew to be true. After all, she kept all her fan mail, and had a special file for her favorites to reread during those days when life wasn't as funny as it should be.

Online—and in just about every other form of mass communication—there was a lot of grumbling, with complaints of fixed votes and bribes and heavy hints of favoritism. Harley could not believe the response. She was in heaven!

After a seemingly endless second day of semifinals, the finalists had been chosen via a panel of secret judges, votes from the Internet audience, and, of course, Harley. Now it was time to drop in on the tech behind her success—the one and only . . .

"Hi, Batgirl!" Harley shouted as she entered the Bat-Bunker. "Any press is good press, don't you think?" she said, tossing her mallet in the air. Just as Harley was about to grab it, a net dropped from the ceiling and caught it. "Hey, that's mine!" she complained.

"It's mine now," Batgirl said good-naturedly. "You know that no one's supposed to play with their weapons in here. I have too much high-tech equipment and can't afford for anything to break. I'll give it back to you when you leave."

Harley wandered around the Bat-Bunker, the dorm room that doubled as Batgirl's computer control center. The screens glowed blue in the purple room.

"So, what are my numbers?" Harley asked, pressing some buttons randomly.

Batgirl removed Harley's hand from her keyboard and reset the computers back to the way they were. Then she flexed her fingers and addressed the computer keyboard like a pianist. Instantly, a detailed map of Metropolis appeared with numbers running across it. Overlaid on top of that, a map of the United States appeared, then a map of the world, then the key locations around the greater galaxy covered the screen. "Take a look for yourself," Batgirl said, scooting over.

Harley leaned in. The number was getting bigger and bigger. "*WOWZA!*" she proclaimed. "I'm a huge hit!"

"Yes, but not everyone is a fan," Supergirl pointed out.

Harley had been so focused on the numbers, she hadn't noticed Supergirl eating cookies in the corner. "Look at your message board."

On another screen were comments from viewers. Most were like this:

> The BEST show ever. I love HQ's
> Dance-O-Rama!
> —Dance-O-Rama Fan Family
>
> Harley Quinn deserves the awesome-
> ness award!"   —MH234
>
> Can't wait to see the finals. I just
> know Beast Boy is going to win!!!
> —Beast Boy

But some said:

> Killer Croc should have been a
> finalist. So what if he's a criminal?
> —KC Fan Club and Employees
>
> The votes were rigged!
> —CAD Academy Parents Association
>
> Watch out, Harley Quinn, you picked
> the wrong dancers!!! —Anonymous

Supergirl wrinkled her brow. "Do those bother you?" she asked.

"Aw, shucks!" Harley said after reading the angry comments. "I'm not afraid of anyone! So what if I lose a couple of viewers? I've got plenty more where they came from!"

With the finals less than a week away, the dance competition was all anyone could talk about. "It's too bad you and Parasite didn't try out," Katana said to Miss Martian.

Miss Martian blushed. "Dancing's not my thing."

"Well, it's *my* thing," Star Sapphire said. She pirouetted around the tables in the dining hall, hitting several students with her deep purple hair as she whirled around. "I've already started planning my victory party."

"Nothing like a little self-doubt," The Flash said to himself as he passed by holding a tray piled high with cheeseburgers.

Sapphire straightened her tiara. "I'm having couture costumes made for me and my corps de ballet. Now all I need is a dance partner." She looked around. "Oh, Flash," she said as she adjusted the glowing ring on her finger. "May I have a word with you?"

Since the dozen finalists included entries from Super Hero High, Wildcat left the gym open for the groups to practice. "Nothing wrong with home court advantage," he said when Hawkgirl asked if this was fair.

"Let's triple-check this," Hawkgirl said to Batgirl.

"I'm all for that," Batgirl said, consulting her computer. "My list includes the following: one hundred Tappers from Tap Dance Town; The CAD Academy Break-Dancers; the Belle Reve Penitentiary Guard Cha-Cha-Chas; Little Beth from Miss Toddler Tot's School for the Tiny and Talented; the Jigs Up, a group of former bank robbers from Limerick, Ireland; the Doomsday Divas, a group of reformed villains; a trio of dancers from Intensity Institute; our own Super Hero High entries; and the mystery dancer."

"Who's the mystery dancer?" Hawkgirl asked. "I don't like not knowing."

"Harley, who's the mystery dancer?" Batgirl asked.

"Don't know," Harley said. "It's a mystery!"

"There's no way we can fit the hundred tap dancers in the gym—and it's a direct violation of the fire code," Hawkgirl noted, shaking her head. "Last time we had them dance in the parking lot. But that's going to be full of vehicles since the competition is a hot ticket."

Batgirl agreed. "What do you want to do about that?"

"I don't know," said Harley. She was editing a commercial featuring the finalists and trying to mimic their moves. "You guys figure out the details. I'm more of a big-picture person."

"Outside," Batgirl said. "They'll have to dance outside on the sports field. I can get Supergirl and some of the others to construct a dance floor—"

"Heard you, and we're already on it!" Supergirl said over Batgirl's comm bracelet. "Look out the window."

Harley could see Supergirl and Wonder Woman carrying twenty-foot stacks of wood planks and handing them off to The Flash, who was building a dance floor at super-speed on the sports field as Bumblebee directed him.

"**WOWZA!** We've thought of everything," Harley enthused. "What could possibly go wrong?"

CHAPTER 7

Saturday morning rolled around sooner than anyone expected. Wonder Woman enjoyed several bowls of colorful sugary cereals—it was her one weakness. Bumblebee fortified her steel-cut oatmeal with extra honey. Batgirl had gotten up early, had fruit, granola, and yogurt, and was already at work in the gym where the show was taking place. A stickler for details, she wanted to triple-check the equipment.

"Can you go faster?" Harley asked. She was so excited that she had eaten breakfast three times. Two on purpose, one by accident.

"I could if you would please move aside," Batgirl said. She was staring into Cyborg's eyes as he stared back at her. "Harley, can you see what he sees?" she asked.

Harley checked her computer. "Yep!" she said gleefully. "What an awesome, incredible idea, to have extra cameras! Who was the genius who thought of that?"

"You," Batgirl said, rolling her eyes.

Harley blushed and fanned her face with her hands. "Aww, you are too kind!"

"How do I turn this off?" Cyborg asked. "I don't want everyone to know what I see all the time!"

"Just blink quickly three times to turn it off, four to turn it on," Batgirl told him.

Harley batted her eyes at him. "Thanks, Cyborg! Be sure to get the crowd shots. The ones of them cheering and yelling. Oh, and lots of shots of the host, too."

"That's you, Harley," he said, imitating Batgirl good-naturedly.

Harley tapped the side of his metal head. "Nothing gets past you, does it?" she joked.

"Bumblebee, just in time. You're next," Batgirl said as her friend arrived and shrank down to be outfitted with a micro-camera. That way, she could fly right into the middle of the dancers and broadcast live.

As Harley tested the camera, Batgirl blurted out, "Macro micro mini drone!"

"Whatzat?" asked Harley.

Batgirl shook her head. "Oh, just an idea," she said. "I'll tell you later. You've got a show to put on. Plus, you've got to coordinate with all the judges."

"The judges?" Harley asked.

"I know you had help selecting the semifinalists, so I assumed you'd have judges for the finals," Batgirl said.

Harley's brain was racing. She knew there was something she'd forgotten. "Snap!" she finally said. "Here's a news flash: no finalist judges. I've got something a billion times better!"

"What?" Batgirl asked.

"Me!" said Harley, nodding happily. "I can't wait to name the winner! Excuse us—the judges have some decisions to make."

After conferring with herself, Harley decided that she alone would determine who the winner was. After all, this was her Web channel, and this was her show.

The dance-off started smoothly. Star Sapphire and her corps de ballet were marvelous. After Barda made sure all the loudspeakers were working, she played the music from Tchaikovsky's *Swan Lake*. The ballerinas' costumes sparkled whenever they pirouetted, which was often. Then, when The Flash lifted Sapphire, he paused so the audience could take in the beauty of his partner—that was her idea.

"Spin!" Star Sapphire whispered. "Like we practiced."

The Flash nodded, started off slowly, and then spun so fast

the two of them rose in the air, to the delight of the audience. Then, as they floated above, purple glitter showered down on the crowd. Never had there been louder cheering, or more sparkles, for Swan Lake.

As if to balance the beauty and grace of Sapphire's dance team, CAD Academy went next. Captain Cold was in charge, as usual. He swaggered up onstage, followed by his crew: Ratcatcher and Magpie. While Barda manned the DJ booth and played the hard-driving beat, Captain Cold and company jerked around in an odd but mesmerizing rhythm.

"Cap'n Cold and His Break-Dancers are in the house!" Barda yelled as Captain Cold pulled a plate out of his jacket and hurled it at the audience.

A roar of approval went up as the CAD Academy dancers broke dozens of dishes—smashing them on the ground, and throwing them into the audience and at each other.

At the far end of the gym, Parasite looked on and shook his head. He knew who would be cleaning up the mess.

"They crack me up," Harley said with a laugh as she took center stage while the CAD Academy students took their bows.

The show continued at whiplash pace, with Harley at the helm and Cyborg and Bumblebee displaying stellar camera work. "Next," Harley announced, "we go outside for the One Hundred Tappers, and not one of them is under one hundred years old! You know what that means, right? One hundred times one hundred equals awesome!"

The special dance floor that Supergirl and the others had installed worked perfectly. The sound of two hundred feet tapping in unison was so loud it could be heard in Metropolis and beyond. The crowd was so jazzed by the tapping tones of the 100 Tappers that they stood up and began tapping along. When the Super Hero High buildings began to shake off their foundations, Harley was forced to cut their dance short. Even she was worried that they might cause an earthquake.

"**WHOA** and **WOWZA!** That's going to be a hard act to beat," Harley said as she led the audience back inside. "But now we have a team who teaches by day and dances by night—our very own Super Hero High teachers!"

The audience oohed as the lights dimmed and a disco ball lowered from the ceiling. When Supergirl's laser gaze hit the mirrored ball, it lit up and showered the gym with hundreds of thousands of reflective sparkles. When Barda dropped the needle on a disco classic, Crazy Quilt struck a pose, looking resplendent in his all-white three-piece suit with flared pants and oversized purple glasses. His body moved in a combination of quick jerks and fluid spins. He did the splits—*literally*—and leapt up, not letting the rip in his pants stop him. When Vice Principal Grodd appeared behind Crazy Quilt along with June Moone, the music veered as the two did a graceful modern dance depicting the beauty of the change of seasons.

"**YOWZA,** will ya look at that!" Harley exclaimed.

Now the trio locked arms and were doing a high kick ending with a three-person backflip. The audience was on their feet cheering as the teachers left the stage.

"A-plus!" shouted Harley.

Someone was pacing behind Barda. When Harley called him onto the stage, she was surprised to hear him say into the mic, "Golly gosh, I'm so nervous." He was green, but then, he always was. "I don't think I can do this!"

Beast Boy looked like he was on the verge of tears. The audience sat silent. A few even sobbed along with him as the green teen buried his face in his hands and wept. He started to walk off stage, defeated before he had even begun.

"Aww, Beasty, you're gonna be great," Harley assured him.

"You know what?" Beast Boy looked around at the crowd. "You're right!" He gave one of his impish grins, pointed to Big Barda, and yelled, "Hit it, BB!"

As the music pulsated, Beast Boy morphed into an astonishing menagerie of animals. A hip-hop hippo, a graceful gazelle, a belly-dancing anaconda, and a twisting, turning otter. He had morphed through thirty-seven different animals by the time he was done. It took both Supergirl and Katana to get Beast Boy off the stage. As he took his umpteenth bow, Harley leapt over him to the center of the stage.

"And now for our mystery group," she announced. Harley paused for drama. She was all about the drama. "This last-minute addition has been together since they met at Pedigree Prep Hall in kindergarten. Having just graduated from high school, they are looking for their next adventure. Perhaps it will be as professional dancers? You tell me! Put your hands together for a group you're going to be hearing a lot from . . . the Green Team!"

The gym went dark. Slowly the lights went back on and, through a haze of smoke, the Green Team seized the stage. The young men and women were dressed in chic matching designer suits.

"They're wearing Calder Melino shoes!" Sapphire whispered appreciatively to Lady Shiva as she took a picture of them and instantly posted it on #FashionistaFotos.

With precision so sharp that the entire audience gasped as if on cue, the Green Team snapped into three rows of four. They bowed and began to dance to the sounds of Celtic fusion funk. Acting as one instead of twelve, the Green Team incorporated all the styles of dance that been displayed in the contest thus far into their own performance.

"This is truly amazing," Harley said breathlessly. "We are seeing the future of dance! Green Team, we're expecting to see a lot of you in the future!"

The audience was on their feet roaring their approval.

"Next up, we name the winners," Harley announced. "But first, a short break!"

"I dunno, I dunno," Harley wailed as she nervously yanked on her own bouncy blond pigtails.

"You dunno what?" Barda asked.

"I dunno who the winner is," Harley said to herself. "They are all *sooo* good!"

"True," Batgirl agreed. "But you have to pick one. Remember, instead of audience votes or a secret ballot, you said you were going to be the sole judge."

"Is it too late to do an online audience vote?" Harley asked, biting her fingernails.

Batgirl nodded. "You have to go out there now and announce the winner. This show is streaming live. Your audience is waiting."

Harley grimaced and pulled on her pigtails even harder.

"Quiet, everyone!" Harley yelled.

Outside, one hundred tap dancers stood at attention. Cyborg aimed his camera on them in case they were the winners. Inside, Grodd, Crazy Quilt, and June Moone held hands, waiting to hear their names. The CAD Academy break dancers were already congratulating themselves, and Sapphire had changed into her new celebration party dress as The Flash tried in vain to remove the purple glitter from his costume.

"This is a first!" Harley said, her excitement bubbling up as she thought out loud. "Never before in the entire history of dance contests has something like this ever happened!"

The Green Team looked at each other and tried not to smile. Little dancing toddlers from Miss Toddler's Tots School for the Talented and Tiny squirmed in their mothers' arms. The Wally Waltzers from Vienna held their collective breath.

"The winner is . . . EVERYONE!" Harley cried. "It's a twelve-way tie!"

The audience was silent. Stunned. Then the noise began. It was unclear whether people were cheering or booing, but either way, Harley was happy.

"And that's it for the first-ever Harley's Dance-O-Rama. Tune in for my next totally live, totally unexpected contest. Until then, keep watching. I know I will be!"

The cameras shut off, but the crowd remained. Some were

applauding the audacity of it all. Others were grumbling. And others were getting louder as they expressed their displeasure, since they were certain their team or their favorite should have been the one and only winner.

"I won?" Beast Boy asked, looking confused. "But so did they?" he pointed to the trio from CAD Academy. They looked more intimidating than usual, if that was possible.

"We should have been the sole winners." Captain Cold's voice was as chilly as ice. He started to freeze Harley, but Wonder Woman stopped him with her lasso.

"This is a travesty," Sapphire said, staring down Harley. "I should have won! I've already paid for the party!"

"But you did win," Harley sputtered, unsure of why some people were mad at her. "Everyone won."

"It's not winning if there are others on the winner's stand," Sapphire lectured Harley. "If this is your idea of a joke, it isn't funny!"

When Harley started to protest, Cheetah commented, "Looks like the class clown has really flubbed this one."

Despite the mixed reactions to Harley's announcement, or maybe because of it, her viewership soared. Not only did a record number of people tune in, but they watched the Dance-O-Rama over and over again. Harley was getting hundreds of messages at a time. She was loving it.

"*Unexpected* was the word for Harley Quinn's first-ever dance contest," Lois Lane reported. "The chatter is burning up the Internet. Some are thrilled with the judicious twelve-way tie. Others are incensed, saying that Harley copped out by refusing to name one winner. There have even been threats lobbed at her. Harley, what do you have to say about all this?"

Harley smiled at the camera. "I say let's do it again. But first, I've got something even bigger planned. You'll be the third to know, Lois. First me, when I think of it. Second will be my loyal and loving Harley's Quinntessentials audience!"

"Harley, are you worried about the angry comments?" Lois asked. "Some dance fans can get pretty serious."

"Nah," she said, sounding cavalier. "I can handle anything. I'm Harley Quinn!"

CHAPTER 8

At the weekly assembly, Supers were flying and tumbling and climbing the walls. That is, until Principal Waller took the stage and cleared her throat. Instantly, everyone was seated and the room was so silent you could hear Vice Principal Grodd crack his knuckles. Repeatedly.

As Waller congratulated the Dance-O-Rama competitors from Super Hero High, the dancers stood to be acknowledged. The reception was thunderous. After all, the Supers were always ready to support each other. Star Sapphire and her corp, including The Flash, stood and twirled before taking a bow. Beast Boy turned into a parrot and flew overhead squawking, "Thank you! Thank you! Thank you!" And the teachers waved politely, as if they were in a parade.

"Disco! Disco! Disco!" the Supers chanted. It didn't take much for Crazy Quilt to stand and strike a disco pose.

"You do the disco pose!" a Super yelled to Principal Waller. Harley looked around to see who would be so brave.

No one was taking credit.

"Never going to happen," Principal Waller said, trying to hide her amusement. "Now, let's talk about why you are all here and the responsibilities you shoulder."

Big Barda had a piece of lemon cake in front of her, but she was ignoring it.

"You gonna eat that?" Harley asked. She loved cake. Birthday cakes. Pound cakes. Funnel cakes. Ice cream cakes. All cakes—especially cakes right in front of her!

"Not hungry. You can have it," Barda said, handing it over.

As Harley dug in, Supergirl put her arm around Barda's shoulder. "Are you all right? You look worried."

"I think Principal Waller was talking about me," Barda said, staring down at her lap.

"What do you mean?" Bumblebee asked. She was working on her second slice of honey bread.

"I think that when she was talking about responsibility, she was telling me that I'm responsible for Granny Goodness and the Female Furies when they came through the Boom Tubes and tried to take over the school," Big Barda said in a rush.

"Well, you were one of them then," Harley said, trying to be helpful.

Supergirl, Bumblebee, Thunder, and Lightning glared at her.

"Wha?" Harley said through a mouthful of cake. "It's true!"

Supergirl turned back to Barda. "That was then. You've changed and helped the fight against evil and are partly responsible for our victories!"

"That's right," Lightning chimed in. "Remember what Principal Waller keeps telling us?

" 'We are here because of who we can become tomorrow,' " her sister said.

Supergirl nodded. "I didn't ask for my powers of strength and flight and heat vision. But now that I have them, I have a responsibility to make sure I use them to my best ability, and to help others in the process. Harley," she said, "what's your take on responsibility?"

Harley polished off the last morsel of cake and the colorful crumbs left on the plate. "I've been giving this lots and lots of thought," she told the group. "So many thoughts, my noggin' is a-swimming. Ha! Can you just picture a head swimming?"

Everyone waited for Harley to sit down and stop pretending that her head had come free and was bobbing up and down on an imaginary ocean.

"Anyway," she continued. "I was thinking about the Dance-O-Rama and how great it was, and even now the replays of the Web special are getting more and more views. Plus, I got a record number of comments after—"

Miss Martian leaned over and whispered reverently to Ivy, "She gets tons of fan mail! I know. I've seen it."

"—so when I think about responsibility, I think that it is my responsibility to . . . Are you ready? This is big!" Everyone nodded as Harley stood on her chair and shouted, "It is my responsibility to announce that the next Harley's Quinntessentials will feature . . . a Battle of the Bands!"

CHAPTER 9

"Who can tell us why your weapons are important?" Mr. Fox asked. He strolled purposefully up and down the rows of desks with his hands laced behind his back. His thick black glasses made him look serious, but his orange sweater and magenta tie said otherwise.

Wonder Woman raised her hand.

"Yes, Wonder Woman?" the Weapononics teacher said.

"Our weapons are to protect and defend," she began. "However, in the wrong hands they could be used to destroy. It is our responsibility to use them wisely."

"Excellent!" said Mr. Fox, beaming. "Anyone else? Harley, what about your mallet?"

Harley had been daydreaming about the Battle of the Bands. In her imagination, after the winner was announced, she would start a record label called Mallet Music, and it would be an instant hit—

"Harley?" Mr. Fox said, snapping her out of her daydream.

"Huh? Harley? That's my name, don't wear it out!" Harley quipped.

As the class laughed, Mr. Fox shook his head. Harley smiled sheepishly and shrugged.

Unfortunately, this was not the last time she'd be caught daydreaming.

In history class, their teacher Liberty Belle talked about the great battles of the last century—including recent ones with the Supers, led by Katana, battling Dragon King, and Supergirl leading the charge against Granny Goodness, and Batgirl versus the Calculator.

"I seek to honor the legacy of my grandmother," Katana said. "She fought hard against evil, and passed down her beliefs to me. I feel that in my heart."

"Thank you," Liberty Belle said. "Harley, you look like you want to say something. What can you add to this conversation?"

Harley had been poking the girl in front of her, who was doing an excellent job of ignoring her. She was hoping Hawkgirl would agree to be stage manager for the Battle of the Bands.

"Harley . . . ?" Liberty Belle said, waiting for an answer.

"**WOWZA,** Teach!" Harley said, glancing around the

room. "Um, er . . . well, yes." She wished she knew what the question was. That would make things so much easier!

Everyone was staring at her. Cheetah smiled and whispered, "We were talking about our favorite foods."

Harley winked a "thank you" and said with gusto, "Fried pickles and triple-chocolate swirly ice cream loaded with sprinkles!"

Harley had one last class that day. An elective. Music. Super Hero High had been missing a music teacher ever since the last one fled during Thunder and Lightning's Dueling Duets demonstration. Thunder had created powerful shock waves that hit all the acoustic instruments, causing them to reverberate cacophanously. Then Lightning countered by trying to commandeer the electronic synthesizers and drum machines with her electrical powers and overloading them. The equipment began to malfunction and sparks flew—musically and literally.

"I can't wait to meet the new teacher," Harley was saying as she bounced down the hallway.

"Me too!" said Raven as she rushed past, her dark cloak fluttering behind her.

The music room was full. Some students were carrying their instruments—violins, guitars, a piano. Big Barda had an accordion, and Green Lantern was polishing his tuba.

The man in the front of the classroom was bent over, digging through a briefcase. "Ah! Here it is," the new teacher said, pulling out a silver flute. His green cape covered his face, but when he pulled it off, he had a brilliant smile. "I am your new music teacher, Pied Piper!"

"Mr. Pied Piper," Beast Boy called out, "what kind of music will you be teaching?"

"What kind would you like?" he asked, waving his flute like a conductor's baton.

As they called out "Classical!" "Hip-hop!" "Retro rock!" "Jazz!" "New wave!" and "Electrolite!" the Pied Piper nodded.

"We will do all that and more. But first, I've heard a musical rumor. Harley Quinn!" he called out. "Is it true you're putting on a Battle of the Bands? If so, I'd like to offer my services to coach any Super Hero High musicians who might be competing. Is that okay with you?"

Harley grabbed one side of Big Barda's accordion. "Hold on!" she instructed Barda as she ran across the room, stretching out the bellows. "Here's my answer, Mr. Pied Piper, sir!"

She let go and the accordion folded back toward Barda, making a *wooom* sound. "That's music for yes," Harley said, letting go of a big laugh. "This 'battle' is gonna be epic!"

CHAPTER 10

Batgirl was buried. There were so many audition videos and Web links of bands that it was almost a full-time job logging them all in—and it had only been a couple of days since Harley's announcement.

"It's gonna be the biggest and baddest and best-est Battle of the Bands this world has ever seen!" Harley proclaimed to her Web fans. "Everyone is welcome to enter. Just send in a short audition tape, and if you're one of the lucky finalists, you will perform LIVE on the Internet for an audience of a zillion-ish viewers!"

"What can we do to help?" the ever-efficient Hawkgirl asked.

"You can help me log these in," Batgirl said, pushing a pile of old-school tapes and discs toward her.

"Is this why you called a meeting of the Junior Detective Society?" Bumblebee asked. "For our help in sorting this all out?"

The Junior Detective Society was a school club mostly comprised of Batgirl, Hawkgirl, The Flash, and Bumblebee—though other Supers helped them with cases or came to them for help. The Junior Detectives loved a mystery.

"Yep," Batgirl confirmed. "It's a mystery how we can get through the auditions. We need a system to sort and view everything. Harley's putting together a group of Supers and citizens to help listen, right?"

Harley nodded, then went back to watching a commercial of herself advertising the Battle of the Bands on one of Batgirl's computer screens.

"We're on it," Hawkgirl said. She was already drawing a diagram of a sorting system, while The Flash in a nanosecond—or two—had logged in the videos. Meanwhile, Bumblebee was online, scanning the emails with musical Web links.

"It's like anyone who's ever picked up a musical instrument is vying to get on the show!" The Flash exclaimed.

Sure enough, it was a who's who of super heroes, super villains, and citizens. "Look!" Bumblebee called out excitedly. "Mandy Bowin is auditioning!"

Mandy had been a student at Super Hero High, but left to pursue her music. Also on the list was the Korugar Academy Marching Band, plus Black Canary and the Birds of Prey, and the Bad Banshees featuring Silver Banshee on vocals, Gizmo on drums, and Jinx at the keyboard.

"There are lots of Supers from Super Hero High trying out, too!" Hawkgirl noted.

A knock on the Bat-Bunker door interrupted them. Batgirl buzzed Wonder Woman in. "Dinnertime!" said Wonder Woman.

"You guys go ahead," Batgirl said to her friends. "I want to finish this up, then send it out to the preliminary screeners and the judges."

At last the room was quiet, and Batgirl exhaled. "So nice to be alone sometimes!" she said after a few minutes of silence.

"So then," a voice said, "do you think I'll break the number for the most viewers with BOB? That's what I've nicknamed Battle of the Bands. BOB, get it?"

"Harley, you startled me!" Batgirl said, laughing. "I thought you had left with the others."

Harley began randomly touching all the buttons and keys on Batgirl's computer console. "I've asked you not to do that," Batgirl said, moving her friend's hands away. "Was there something you wanted to talk about? Is this about Battle . . . er, BOB?"

"Maybe, maybe not," said Harley. She was now fiddling with Batgirl's Batarang and accidentally dislodged it.

Batgirl ducked, then caught it with one hand while still typing with the other. "What is it?" she asked.

"Aww, nothing!" Harley said, putting on a smile to mask

her frown. "I was just scared for half a second. But it's dumb, and I'm fine. Not to worry. I'm not worried. Who's worried? Not me! Is it you? What are you worried about, Batgirl? Do you wanna talk?"

"Harley, stop jumping on my bed and tell me what's going on," Batgirl said, patiently.

Harley sat cross-legged on the floor and Batgirl joined her.

"What if I mess up?" Harley said, so softly that Batgirl had to strain to hear. "What if the Battle of the Bands isn't a huge hit? Some people are already mad at me because I named everyone a winner at the Dance-O-Rama."

"I thought this sort of thing didn't bother you," Batgirl said.

"It doesn't!" Harley said a little too loudly.

Batgirl didn't respond.

"Okay, okay, it does bother me a little. But don't tell anyone. I have a reputation to uphold!"

"Everyone likes you," Batgirl assured her.

"Not everyone," Harley said. "Some people think I'm just a class clown. But I'm more than that, aren't I?"

Batgirl reached over and gave her a hug. "You're fun and funny, and a super friend. You've proven yourself to be a hero again and again. Harley Quinn, you're one of a kind!"

Harley gave her friend an "aww, shucks" grin as Batgirl turned back to the task at hand.

CHAPTER 11

The Internet was lit up, and rumors were flying so fast about who would make it to the finals that everyone was dizzy. Some of the musicians were even sending promotional items like T-shirts emblazoned with their band's logo on them in the hopes of currying favor with the judges.

"Look! I got this in the mail," Miss Martian said. She was so excited she kept shifting from foot to foot.

Miss Martian unfurled a poster of the Green Team. Inexplicably, they were standing on a white sand beach, each gazing in a different direction, as the orange sun melted into the azure sea. The headline read

FOR YOUR BATTLE OF THE BANDS CONSIDERATION: THE GREEN TEAM!

Clipped to the top of the poster was a twenty-dollar bill.

"That," said Hawkgirl, frowning, "is an infringement upon the rules. No bribes! The Green Team just disqualified themselves."

"Yeah," Harley had to admit. "They're out. That's a shame. Since the Dance-O-Rama they've earned a huge following."

Miss Martian stared dreamily at the Green Team and asked, "Can I keep the poster?"

"We cannot, cannot, cannot have the same mess we had with the twelve-way tie for the Dance-O-Rama," Harley told Batgirl.

"But, Harley, you were the one—" Hawkgirl started to say, but Harley put her fingers in her ears.

"I can't hear you," Harley said. "Lalalalala, I can't hear you!"

"I can program the site so that no one can vote more than once," Batgirl was saying. "I'm installing a pupil recognition device to ensure one person, one vote."

"Well, since you have this under control, I'm off to the Battle of the Bands location," Harley informed them. She was now pacing the room, adding a few flips here and there. "It's spectacular!"

Batgirl looked up. "Where is it?"

"Not sure yet," Harley admitted. "But when I find it, I'll let ya know!"

As Harley and Katana flew in the Invisible Jet with their pilot, Wonder Woman, they looked for a venue that would be inviting, could hold lots of people, and had great acoustics.

The trio was getting weary. Flying around the world was exhausting. So many places to go. So much to see. So little time. They flew over Diamond Head in Hawaii, but there was no guarantee that the volcano wouldn't erupt mid-BOB. The Colosseum in Rome was "too old and musty-dusty," according to Harley, and the Sydney Opera House in Australia was already booked.

"What about the Grand Canyon?" Wonder Woman suggested. She shifted gears and turned her jet ninety-seven degrees to the left. "The acoustics would be amazing!"

Soon they were flying above the South Rim. Red rocks and mile-deep canyons revealed the millions and millions of years of geological history.

"This looks like the perfect place for BOB!" Harley enthused.

As they landed and scrambled out of the jet, Katana looked down into a ravine. "Hello!" she yelled.

"Hello! Hello! Hello!" it answered.

"Too much echo," Katana said, shaking her head.

"Knock, knock!" Wonder Woman said, giving it a try.

"Knock, knock, knock, knock," the Grand Canyon replied,

and then added, "Who's there?"

"Huh!" Wonder Woman shouted. "Did you hear that?"

Harley couldn't stop laughing. "That was me! Okay, where to next?"

"Food?" said Wonder Woman. "I'm hungry."

"Me too," Katana said.

"Me three," Harley agreed.

Wonder Woman shifted into autopilot. After landing near Metropolis's Centennial Park, the girls were on foot when Katana stopped abruptly, causing Harley to bump into her. "Do you hear that?" Katana asked.

"Hear what?" asked Harley. "The laughter of little children at play? The melodic tunes of the birds singing? The plaintive meow of Rainbow the cat up the tree?"

"No," Katana said, pivoting around. "That!"

Wonder Woman was already on the move. Three burly truck drivers were yelling.

"Help!" the biggest one cried. "Our trucks were stolen and they're full of medical equipment for the Metropolis Hospital!"

"We've got this covered!" Harley assured him.

With Wonder Woman in the air and Harley and Katana on

the ground, they caught up to the wayward trucks in no time. Blocking the vehicles, the Supers stood with their hands on their hips as the trucks screeched to a halt only inches away from them.

For a brief second, the smile slid off Harley's face. "Uh-oh," she said.

"Not good," Katana agreed.

"Not good for them," Wonder Woman added.

"Well, hello, hello, girlies," said the criminal, who looked like a cross between a pterodactyl and a man. He flapped his powerful wings, causing the leaves to blow off the trees.

Wonder Woman's eyes narrowed. "Hello, Airstryke."

"How's Queen Hippolyta?" the baddie Airstryke asked as he rose above the ground. "I haven't seen you or your mother since she threw me in prison."

Wonder Woman flew up so they were face to face, one hundred feet in the air.

Harley stood her ground, twirling her mallet, ready for action. Katana was poised to unsheathe her sword.

"Mom's fine, thanks for asking," said Wonder Woman as Airstryke flew at her with his sharp teeth bared. "You should brush more often," she added.

Katana and Harley were about to throw their weapons at him, when the doors of the other trucks flew open. A muscled man who had a skull instead of a face stepped out of one, and a man dressed in red with yellow boots and cape leapt out of the other.

"Aerialist and Atomic Skull," Katana said to Harley. "Liberty Belle told us about them, remember?"

Harley nodded in the affirmative, but in reality she wished she had paid more attention in class.

"I got the leaping guy," Harley called out as Aerialist jumped backward on top of a truck. She tossed her camera up against a nearby building so that it hit the wall . . . and stuck.

Katana crouched down. "Atomic Skull's mine," she said.

As the battle ensued in the air, on the ground, and along the desolate road, Harley was laser-focused on Aerialist.

"You used to be a stuntman?" she asked as he hurled himself toward her.

Harley cartwheeled at him so fast that she was nothing more than a blur of a ball. Midair, she hit him with her mallet. "How's that for a stunt?" she asked. He slammed against a nearby building and then fell to the ground, completely stunned.

Above, Wonder Woman was in fast pursuit of Airstryke, who did a one-hundred-eighty-degree turn in midair and started chasing her. "Wonder Woman, look at you," he said. "I remember when you were just an itty-bitty little thing trailing along in your mother's shadow!"

"Well, Airstryke, I'm not a little girl anymore!" Wonder Woman adjusted the golden cuffs her mother had given her. She lifted her Lasso of Truth and began to twirl it. As it sliced through the air, it was Airstryke's turn to flee.

As Airstryke tried to get away, she lassoed his foot, and with a mighty pull, sent him hurtling toward the ground.

Meanwhile, Atomic Skull began to glow. He was emitting a radioactive field as Katana circled him, sword in hand. "What do you want with the medical equipment?" the villain asked.

"I want to help the children at the hospital," she said.

"Your heart is too soft." He laughed and shook his head.

"Maybe," Katana said, tightening her grip. "But my sword is not!"

A few yards away, Harley bowled the Aerialist over with a swing of her mallet as he leaped toward her. He went soaring when the mallet made contract. Midair, he crashed into Airstryke, and the two villains tumbled onto the asphalt in a heap.

"Now, that's what I call an air strike," Harley said with a laugh.

Flying around the defeated villains at super-speed, Wonder Woman tied them up with the Lasso of Truth. Then she and Harley joined Katana.

"Something's wrong with your noggin!" Harley quipped

as Atomic Skull began generating more and more energy. The heat force around him expanded. "You're getting all full of yourself."

Atomic Skull laughed. "Goodbye, super heroes," he said. "Nice knowing you!"

But before he could activate his lethal blast projection, Harley distracted him with a series of cartwheels. Simultaneously, Katana caught his attention as she neared him with her sword. Atomic Skull didn't see Wonder Woman. The Amazon had picked up a large moving van and scooped him up into the back. The villain was jostled as he banged around inside the truck.

Harley slammed the doors of the van as Wonder Woman set it down. Katana put her sword through the handles to make sure Atomic Skull couldn't get out until the authorities arrived.

"Case closed!" Harley cheered.

CHAPTER 12

By the time Harley and her friends made it to Capes & Cowls, Steve Trevor had a table reserved for them.

"Some truck drivers called and bought these for you," he said. His wide smile revealed his braces as he served the heroes their favorite smoothies.

"Hi, Steve!" Wonder Woman said brightly.

"Hi, Wonder Woman! Um, I have to take some orders, but I'll be back to check on you," he said, backing away and bumping into the table behind him.

"Watch where you're going!" sneered Captain Cold.

"Sorry, sorry," Steve apologized.

Harley was calling Batgirl on her phone. "Would you mind uploading the video I just sent you?" she asked. "It's a Save the Day that just happened."

"Sure thing," Batgirl said from the Bat-Bunker. "I'll also set you up so you'll be able to do it yourself. In the meantime, have you found a venue yet?"

"Still looking," Harley reported. She watched Steve set a huge pizza on the table. One side had ham and pineapple on it, and the other had mushrooms. Harley took two slices of ham and pineapple, put a slice of mushroom between them to make a pizza sandwich, and bit into it.

"We're using the land behind the café as a temporary animal preserve while the zoo gets ready for its new wildlife sanctuary," Steve was telling Katana and Wonder Woman.

"That's nice of you," said Wonder Woman.

"That explains the smell," Harley said, pinching her nose.

"It's no big deal," said Steve. "Anything for the animals. Some have been injured or orphaned, or are old and wouldn't last in the wilderness. If they become strong and independent enough, they're returned to the wild. They'll be out of here and at the sanctuary in a couple days."

Katana looked out the window. She could see the animals milling about. "They've been through a lot. As far as I'm concerned, they can make all the smell and noise they want!"

The table was quiet for a moment as they listened to the animals. It sounded like they were in the same room.

"Hey, Stink-o Steve-o," Ratcatcher called out. "More french fries over here, and make it snappy!" He threw several rat traps on the ground and Steve had to leap over them to avoid getting caught. Snap, snap, snap!

But all Harley could hear was the sounds of the animals.

"Good food. Lots of space. Great acoustics." Harley

began. She looked up at the ceiling as she kept repeating herself. "Good food. Lots of space. Great acoustics. Good food. Lots of space. Great acoustics." Suddenly, Harley leapt to her feet. "I got it! I know where we should hold the Battle of the Bands!"

Steve tiptoed around the rat traps and brought the teens another pie. But instead of a pizza pie, it was an apple pie. "It's made from locally grown apples from Poison Ivy's garden," he said. "Dig in, it's fresh out of the oven."

Steve noticed Harley staring at him . . . very intently.

"Um, is there anything else I can do for you?" he asked.

"You betcha!" Harley said. "You can host my Battle of the Bands here!"

"I don't understand," Steve said. "Here?"

"Here!" said Harley. "You have good food. Lots of space. It's perfect!"

"It is perfect," Wonder Woman chimed in. "We can transform your parking lot and that area where the animals are into an arena. . . ."

"And the café can provide food stands," Katana explained, "and the Supers will help man them. But you can be in charge of the menu, Steve!"

"And your acoustics are awesome," Harley said. She raised her hand and yelled, "Shhh! Everyone be quiet!"

All were silent as they listened to the sound of a green hippopotamus mumbling about needing ice cream.

"What's going on here?" the green hippo said.

"Beast Boy," Harley enthused. "Tell Steve here that Capes and Cowls would be the perfect venue for BOB."

"What she said," Beast Boy said, turning back into a boy.

"Think of the publicity!" Harley added.

"I don't know," Steve said, rubbing his chin thoughtfully. "It's a pretty big deal, the Battle of the Bands. Everyone will be watching."

"Exactly!" Harley said, nodding.

The girls agreed: The café would be just the place. It was centrally located and had everything they were looking for. Plus, the BOB wasn't until after the animals were to be relocated to the zoo's wildlife area.

Just then, the bell on the door signaled another customer. "It's Pied Piper!" Katana said. "Hello!"

The music teacher had been working with the Supers and teachers who had entered the contest, and everyone couldn't help but adore him. Walk past his music room at any hour of the day and you could hear The Flash breaking up more sets of bongos than he was willing to admit, and the retro-rock sounds of Teacher Teacher with Liberty Belle singing lead and backed up by Doc Magnus on the synthesizer and Red Tornado on the electric guitar. And no one could ignore—

or stand—the vivacious vocal stylings of Beast Boy.

"Pied Piper is the best!" Harley was saying as she watched him nodding his head to the music playing on the jukebox.

"Yes, and he's deaf and uses that to his advantage," Katana added.

Harley raised her eyebrows.

Pied Piper waved at the girls as he picked up his to-go order and left.

"Deaf? No way!" Harley insisted. "But he's the music teacher!"

"And an incredible one," Katana added. "Pied Piper can feel the music in a much more powerful way than the rest of us. Plus, the rumor is that he can read lips so well the government has used him as a spy since he also understands several languages!"

"How did I miss that?" Harley asked.

"You've been busy," Katana said. "Harley, sometimes you're so busy you don't notice what's happening around you, or even have time to spend with your friends."

Wonder Woman nodded. "It's true!"

Harley wondered if her friends were trying to tell her something. She made a note to talk to them about it, when she had more time. Then she burst out laughing. *Like, when am I ever going to have more time?* she asked herself.

There were so many students clogging the corridors that Principal Waller asked the head hall monitor to add extra hours.

"Keep it moving," Hawkgirl said as she flew up and down the flight lanes that flanked the walkways. "Nothing to see here!"

"But everything to listen to," quipped Harley as she stood outside the music room. "It's sounding great in there."

She was right. Pied Piper had helped whip the musical acts into shape. Many of them had been good, but under his direction, now they were great.

"Less feedback on the keyboard amp!"

"Your falsetto is sounding false!"

"Love the harmony, keep it up!"

"Dueling pianos, I want more ritardando!"

The only time the competitors weren't listening to him was when they were arguing among themselves.

"As lead singer, I should be able to pick the song," Liberty Belle was saying to Red Tornado.

"Well, it better have a great acoustic guitar solo," he countered.

"Cheetah, could you do your warm-ups over there?" The Flash asked as he broke another pair of bongos. "You're distracting me."

"No, you move," she said, raising her voice.

"Miss Martian? Miss Martian, are you with us?" asked Poison Ivy.

"I'm here," the shy invisible alien said quietly as a cello made its way across the room.

"I could stand here listening all day," said Harley as she looked in from the doorway and waved to her friends.

"And I could write you up," Hawkgirl said good-naturedly. "Anyway, shouldn't you be working on that assignment for Fox's class? It's due tomorrow."

Harley tried to hide her surprise. "Oh! It's due tomorrow? Good thing I'm almost done. Um. Could you remind me just what we're supposed to do?"

The truth was, Harley was so busy with Battle of the Bands that her schoolwork had begun to slip. And so had her time with her friends, and most everything else. On the plus side, her viewership was rising at a rocket's pace. BOB updates were rotated at regular intervals, and then viewers stayed for Harley's exclusive Super Hero High gossip clips and laughed along to reruns of "Super Heroes' Super Blunders."

Luckily, Harley's team of BOB volunteer judges had winnowed the thousands of auditions down to the final fifty. Harley herself would pick the top ten, but she was having trouble deciding. Every audition sounded like a winner, and she had difficulty rejecting anyone because that might make them sad.

"Please pass your assignments to the front of the class," Mr. Fox said. "I am looking forward to reading these. As a preview, we will go around the room and each of you will provide a one-sentence summary of your report. Ms. Quinn, we'll start with you."

Harley gulped and looked desperately at Miss Martian, trying to get her attention. *Read my mind, Miss Martian! Read my mind, and tell me what to say!* Harley had her eyes screwed shut and was thinking hard. *Whisper what the assignment was and what I should say!*

"Harley, are you okay?" Mr. Fox's brows were knit together as he scrutinized her face.

Harley unscrewed her eyes. She looked at Miss Martian, who refused to meet her gaze. "Yes, sir, Mr. Fox, sir!" Harley said.

"And your sentence would be . . . ?" he prodded.

"Well, my report is about all that stuff that is so important and that we need to know about and that we were supposed to write about. And that's what my report is about!" she said.

"Please stay after class, Ms. Quinn," Lucius Fox said. "Now, Wonder Woman, please put your hand down. Yes, you can go next."

"So then he tells me that not only do I have to make up my missing assignment, but I need to write an additional paper on the Power of Powers," Harley said, moaning.

"I can help you with your homework," Supergirl volunteered. A group of girls was hanging out in Harley's room.

"Would you?" Harley said, sitting on the clothes on top of the books on top of her bed. It was hard to tell where the pile ended and the bed began, but that never seemed to bother Harley. "That would be swell! Could you have it done by Tuesday?"

"I said I would help, not do it for you," Supergirl said, sounding friendly but firm.

"But I'm sooo busy with the Battle of the Bands," Harley explained. "We have less than a week to go!"

"Don't I know it?" Supergirl said. She was on Harley's amphitheater committee along with Wonder Woman and The Flash. They were charged with creating a band shell now that the temporary wildlife sanctuary had been moved out.

"Pleeeeease," Harley begged.

"No!" Supergirl replied.

Harley looked exasperated and blew a wisp of hair out of her eyes. "Fine. Homework. Check. Moving on. What's everyone else up to?"

The food committee was headed up by Steve Trevor. Wonder Woman had volunteered to be on that committee, too, as well as on the parking lot committee and the crowd control committee. With Hawkgirl as stage manager, Batgirl was assigned to check in the contestants. Big Barda was in charge of the sound system. And Bumblebee was talent wrangler. The entire Capes & Cowls Café was the designated greenroom. With the waiting area sure to be packed, Bumblebee's ability to shrink made her the ideal candidate to weave in and out of the crowd of hopefuls.

"A greenroom is just what they call where the talent hangs out before they go onstage," Batgirl explained. She knew this, having been a contestant on TechTalk TV.

"But it's not green," Poison Ivy pointed out. "Though I could fix that."

Suddenly Harley leapt up and began jumping on her bed, holding her hands up so she wouldn't hit her head on the ceiling. "It's time! It's time!"

"What's time?" Ivy asked.

"I'm going live in ten minutes to name the finalists," Harley blurted out. "This is gonna be big! Maybe the biggest thing ever!"

As Harley turned on her video equipment, Big Barda stopped in. "Hey, Harley, me and some of the others are starting a glee club. I'm thinking of calling it Mighty Melody

Makers. Wanna join us? It'll be fun!"

"Fun! Who has time for fun?" Harley said, looking serious, then grinning ear to ear. "I'm about the make the big announcement and I barely have time to eat and sleep. There's no time for glee!"

Adam Strange and Arrowette were hard at work in Centennial Park. Since Harley anticipated overflow crowds, video screens were sent for. That way, spectators could watch off-site and still be a part of the festive atmosphere.

Adam was in the air, hovering with the power of his jet pack. "Is it straight?" he asked, holding up the last giant screen that needed to be placed.

"A little to your left," Arrowette said. She pulled three arrows from her quiver in quick succession, took aim, and shot. Each arrow made a satisfying twang when she let go. They stopped an inch from Adam's hand and secured the screen to the wooden post.

"Hey, you almost hit me," he called out.

Arrowette reached over her shoulder for another arrow from her quiver. "If I wanted to hit you, I would have," she said with a wink.

CHAPTER 13

Harley couldn't stop moving or talking. "Thisisgonnabesobig! Iwouldn'tbesurprisedifIbustedtheInternetwithsomany viewers!" she said as she cartwheeled backstage.

"You're going to have to slow down if you want to be understood," Hawkgirl barked. The amphitheater was still under construction, but it was taking the shape of a giant open oyster shell. Katana had painted the impressive red-and-gold Battle of the Bands sign that hung overhead. Harley had asked her to add her HQ logo, and with the help of art teacher June Moone, Katana created one in neon lights.

For the stage itself, Poison Ivy had suggested that they reuse the dance floor. However, Hawkgirl pointed out that it was pocked and damaged due to one hundred tap dancers and various others.

"Besides," Harley was quick to remind everyone, "this is gonna be BIGGER than the last special, and *YOWZA!*

We need lots and lots and lots of room for the live audience!"

Poison Ivy gave this some thought and absentmindedly began braiding her long red hair before proclaiming, "I've got it! Let's use recycled wood from the old Schumacher Shoelace factory that was recently torn down!"

She had barely finished her sentence when Wonder Woman and Supergirl were on the job. Not only did they think this was a great idea, but later they even stacked boulders they had recently cleared from an avalanche in Denver to flank the sides. For extra oomph, Poison Ivy created a cascade of fragrant flowers and then a huge canopy of tulip trees, saucer magnolias, and ropey vines to shade the audience. The result was spectacular, like nature herself was the architect.

Steve Trevor had several Capes & Cowls Café booths set up around the perimeter. Some sold tropical fruit and berry smoothies, others featured freshly baked cookie crisps in the shapes of musical instruments, and still others sold pizza, veggie burgers, and sweet potato fries. Each booth was manned by volunteers from the zoo and students from Super Hero High. Since the proceeds were going to the wildlife sanctuary, Principal Waller had offered community service points to those who helped out.

"The contestants are starting to arrive," Bumblebee reported from the greenroom. "Ukulele United from the island of Kauai is here and they're passing out fresh orchid leis to everyone. They smell lovely."

"Got it!" Hawkgirl said into her headset. She turned to Harley. "One hour to showtime!"

The Capes & Cowls Café greenroom looked the same as the restaurant always did: cozy and comfortable, yet with a trendy edge to it. The only difference was that Katana had created several posters, one for each of the finalists, with their names and Welcome! on them.

"We're better-looking than that," Captain Cold said, sending a chill around the room. "Well, I am. Not so sure about them." He laughed as other members of CAD Academy's heavy-metal band hauled in their instruments.

Magpie, the drummer, was dressed in a tattered black dress anchored with steel-tipped boots. Ratcatcher had spiked his hair so that it stood up in every direction and could have doubled as a weapon. Captain Cold wore ice-blue mirrored sunglasses and a distressed leather bomber jacket with CC on the back.

"Hey!" Harley yelled at Ratcatcher. Big Barda stood behind her and crossed her arms. "Stop tearing the other groups' posters down or ya get disqualified." She turned to the camera and when the red light went on, Harley began, "In a short while we'll go behind the scenes of HQ's first-ever

Battle of the Bands. And at the top of the hour, stay tuned for the live competition where you, the Internet viewers, have a front-row seat!"

She was grateful that Batgirl had created a portable video control console so that she could record, broadcast, and even edit her shows from anywhere. And the best part was that the whole thing could fit in her pocket!

As the other musicians entered, Beast Boy, whom Harley had designated as the official greeter, welcomed everyone with a "Hello! Hello! Congratulations on making it to the finals!" Then, with her trademark efficiency, Batgirl logged them in. Finalists included Female Furies' Apokopella group with Mad Harriett as the lead, a marching band from Korugar Academy, and Black Canary and the Birds of Prey. Soloists included former Super Hero High student Mandy Bowin on violin, and current Super Hero High student Cheetah, who, in an uncharacteristically low-key move, had not made a big deal about her singing.

"I'm going to catch everyone off-guard," she confided to Sapphire, who nodded her approval, "and knock 'em over when they hear me sing."

The contestants eyed each other. Some looked nervous, like Mandy, but most were supremely confident, bordering on belligerent.

"Oops!" said Mad Harriett as she pushed her unruly green hair off her orange face and "by accident" spilled apple juice onto Silver Banshee. "Sorry about that."

Silver Banshee grabbed a napkin and wiped the fruit juice off her costume. Her fluorescent blue pupils began to glow, and her skin flushed briefly before turning pale white again.

"Tell me it was an accident," Silver Banshee said. Her bandmates stood behind her, frowning.

Female Furies Stompa and Speed Queen stood behind Mad Harriett. All grinned menacingly.

Big Barda, who had once been a Fury, stepped between the feuding bands. "No fighting, please."

"Did someone say fighting?" Captain Cold asked. He whipped out his ice blaster and covered the whole café with icicles.

"That's cold," Cheetah said, racing around and breaking the icicles as members of Korugar Academy's band marched over them, making crunching noises.

"Ouch! Hey, watch it!" Ratcatcher squealed when he was accidentally stomped on.

Soon mayhem broke loose as musical instruments flew. When Mandy Bowin retreated to a corner booth, Barda hurried to protect her. "I'll keep you safe," she promised. "By the way, I'm a big fan. Your music has meant so much to me. It's beautiful and soothing and happy."

"Thank you," Mandy said, cradling her violin and ducking nanoseconds before a pizza would have hit her head.

"Contestants! Please cease!" Silver Banshee said. When

everyone ignored her, she raised her voice to supersonic levels. "STOP. NOW."

The whole room rattled. Everyone looked startled and covered their ears.

The room went quiet.

"Thank you," Silver Banshee said. A sly smile crossed her face. "We'll fight it out on the stage."

Harley basked in the applause. As it washed over her, she felt like she was home. "Harley! Harley! Harley!" the audience chanted. Each time the curtains of flowers behind her billowed, it sent out a fragrant scent so lovely, no one would have known that just days before, wild animals had congregated there.

"Aww, you guys!" Harley said, looking out over the massive crowd. "I CAN'T HEAR YOU!" She cupped her ears. "And what about y'all watching from Centennial Park? I can't hear you either!"

As the roars from the two crowds meshed, creating a tsunami of sound, Hawkgirl said into the headset, "Harley, we're ready to go. Announce the first contestant."

Harley cleared her throat. This was her moment. A chance to redeem herself from those who were mad at her for the twelve-way tie at the Dance-O-Rama. A chance to become a force to be reckoned with in the entertainment industry. A chance to become the most watched Internet star ever. She was ready.

"Good afternoon, everyone!" Harley shouted. "Aww, look at all of you. Sit down, sit down. Now stand up, now sit down." Everyone followed along, laughing. "Thank you for coming to Harley's Quinntessentials Battle of the Bands! Our first contestants hail from CAD Academy. Give it up for the heavy metal sounds of Cap'n Cold and Crew!"

As Captain Cold smirked his way onstage, the audience cheered. Heavy metal had never sounded so fresh, so cool, so crisp, so . . . heavy. Even traditionalists like Crazy Quilt were jumping up and down in the aisles. The band finished to uproarious applause.

"Remember Cap'n Cold and Crew when you vote after the show," Harley said. "And remember, you only get one vote, so make it count."

Everyone cheered again. Harley beamed. She wondered if her parents were watching.

"And now we're going to take it down a notch, or two, or three. Just listen to the violin serenade of Mandy Bowin—or as some call her, Virtuoso!"

Mandy looked small. She wore a simple peach-colored dress with a Peter Pan collar and pink ballet slippers. Her brown hair was held in place by a light blue headband.

The audience stirred nervously. How could this girl, a mere mortal, even begin to compete with all the heavy metal that had just exited the stage?

With her eyes closed, Mandy lifted her violin and tucked it snugly under her chin, then gracefully lifted the bow in the air. No one was prepared for what happened next.

It was as if a soothing breeze blew across the amphitheater, sailed over the crowd watching in Centennial Park, and then swept into the new wildlife sanctuary at the zoo. As the musical notes from Mandy Bowin's violin alighted over the audiences and animals, all agreed they had never heard music this beautiful.

"I'm not crying, you're crying," Beast Boy said to Cyborg.

"I'm not crying, she's crying," Cyborg said.

"I'm not crying, he's crying," Frost said, pointing to Vice Principal Grodd as she whisked icicles from her face.

Harley captured it all on camera. She knew that tears and fears were two things that audiences loved, and the tears were flowing.

The smile on Mandy's face was as serene as her music. Suddenly it didn't matter that she wasn't a super hero. When Mandy Bowin played her last note, the audience sat enraptured. It was Beast Boy who leapt to his feet first, followed by thousands of others. The cheering more than doubled the decibels of the heavy metal band. Even Ratcatcher was on his feet cheering, until Captain Cold hit him with a chilly blast.

After several bows, Mandy sheepishly walked off the stage. She grinned at Wonder Woman, who had been standing in the wings. "Virtuoso," Wonder Woman whispered.

As the camera lingered on the two, Harley informed her audience, "Mandy was once a student at Super Hero High, but left to pursue her dream to become a musician. At the same time, Wonder Woman left Paradise Island to pursue her dream to become the best super hero she could be. Talk about amazing second acts! And now we pause for this important message."

While Steve Trevor explained that all the profits from the food venues would go to the zoo's new wildlife sanctuary, Harley readied for the next group.

"This is going great, isn't it?" she said to her crew.

Batgirl, Hawkgirl, and Barda all nodded. It was going well. Smoother than anyone could have imagined.

When Steve was done, there was a polite round of applause led by Wonder Woman. Then Harley cartwheeled back onstage. "Is this on?" she said, playfully tapping the microphone. "Next up, it's a little bit of rock, a little bit of folk, a little bit of rap—and it's all amazing music. Let's say aloha to Ukulele United, the all-ukulele band from the island of Kauai!"

Cheers rose and hands went up in the air as the group from Hawaii hula-danced onto the stage, throwing lush leis of orchids into the crowd. Then, with a single string from a single ukulele, the music began. One at a time, the others joined in, until, united in music, the lead singer launched into a heartwarming ballad about the Hawaiian islands.

Just as Ukulele United were rising to the crescendo, Bumblebee flew onstage, grew full-sized, and took the microphone.

"What are you doing?" Harley yelled. "We're live!"

"Sorry," Bumblebee said to Ukulele United, "but I have to do this." She faced the audience. "This is an emergency. Audience members, we're going to need you to get to a safe place. All Supers in the vicinity, we have to Save the Day! Animals from the zoo and wildlife sanctuary are on the loose and on a rampage!"

The crowd began to panic. Supergirl, Cheetah, and the others tried to calm nerves as they led the crowd to safety, which was quite an effort, considering the thousands of panicked people there.

Harley turned to the camera and reported, "We interrupt this incredible and popular Harley's Quinntessentials Battle of the Bands with this important announcement. There's chaos at the Metropolis Zoo—and so we super heroes gotta go Save the Day!"

"What's the scoop?" Harley asked as she arrived on the scene. Lois Lane was stationed next to an open cage.

"The villain Lion-Mane has released all the animals. They're running wild," Lois informed her.

"Who's running wild, the people or the animals?" Harley asked.

"Both!" said Lois. "Everyone's in a panic!"

"That's not like them," said Beast Boy.

"The animals are normally well taken care of," Poison Ivy chimed in.

"We'll get to the bottom of this," said Wonder Woman, who was flying overhead. "But first, let's make sure everyone is safe!"

As animals and people ran past, Bumblebee buzzed in and said, "I've got a lock on Lion-Mane. He's headed toward the Metropolis Museum of Art."

"Of course!" Batgirl said, looking at her wrist computer. "A new exhibit is going to open tomorrow featuring a priceless jeweled lion statue. It's worth millions!"

"The animals on the loose are a decoy—and they're also meant to be a distraction," Hawkgirl deduced.

"Precisely," added The Flash.

"Camera off," Batgirl said to Harley.

"Aww," Harley moaned. "Think of the viewers!"

"I'm thinking of how to sneak up on Lion-Mane," said Batgirl. "And sneak means he can't know that we know. C'mon, we have a lion to tame!"

While Harley and the others rushed to the museum, the other Supers, led by Beast Boy, rounded up the animals and made sure that frightened citizens were safe.

Batgirl checked in with Supergirl, who informed her, "Beast Boy says that Lion-Mane told the animals that they were all going to be shipped away to desolate desert islands. That unless they ran away, they would no longer be cared for. They panicked."

"That makes sense," said Bumblebee. "The animals are usually so kind and loving. And the zookeepers treat them like family, and vice versa."

"Well, this family is outta control," said Hawkgirl. "The wrong information can do that."

With super-speed and stealth, Harley and the Junior

Detectives approached the museum. The guards were nowhere to be seen. The museum stood eerily empty.

Batgirl consulted her holographic museum map. It glowed green in the air in front of her. "He's there," she said, pointing. "Where the red light is glowing. It senses body heat. Several people are locked in what looks like a storage room. They must be the missing guards."

"They'll be safer there," Hawkgirl noted. "I'll take the north hallway. The rest of you take the stairs and employee elevators. We need to sneak up on Lion-Mane."

"I'll go with you!" Harley said, turning on her camera.

The Flash gave her a stern look. "If your viewers can see what we're up to, so can Lion-Mane. You can't have that on."

"Aww, you're no fun," Harley chided him. But she turned off the camera.

CHAPTER 14

As Harley powered down her camera, the other Supers shifted into stealth mode and scattered in search of Lion-Mane. Harley had just looked up when she saw Beast Boy's shadow. "Smart move!" she said, nodding appreciatively. "You're looking like a lion. He's a lion. Lion versus lion." For good measure, she added, "ROAR!"

"ROAR!" came back at her. Only this one shook the walls.

"Beast Boy?" Harley asked as someone else stepped out of the shadows.

It was Lion-Mane, and he was carrying the famous, fabulous, bejeweled lion sculpture. "**YOWZA,** you got a mighty roar, Mr. Mane," she said, reaching for her mallet. "Have you ever thought about auditioning for the Battle of the Bands as a singer?"

"You better get out of my w— Uh, do you really think I have a great roar?" Lion-Mane asked as he loosened his grip on the statue. He was distracted by her compliment and the thought of performing. "Really? Be honest."

"Oh, sure," Harley said, taking a step back. "But first, you gotta think about this."

With that, she lifted her mallet high and, with all her might, brought it down on his foot. Surprised, Lion-Mane dropped the statue and roared so loud the building rocked, alerting all the Supers.

After Lion-Mane's capture, rain had put a damper on the contest. And with the amphitheater being outdoors, even good intentions couldn't stop the storms.

"We'll reschedule!" Harley proclaimed as the rain threatened to wash her away. But several contestants couldn't make it back the following week, so Harley was forced to scrap the show.

"The good news is that even though the Battle of the Bands was canceled, we still made money for the wildlife sanctuary," Steve Trevor said as he gingerly picked up some wayward rat traps left behind by CAD Academy. It didn't look good for a café to have those lying around.

"That is good news," Harley agreed while she checked her messages. She had gotten several comments about how the BOB had ended. Many said the show should have gone on. However, MH234 wrote: "The best Battle of the Bands in history! Love how it didn't end so that we have something to look forward to on your channel!"

Harley knew she could always count on MH234 to cheer her up.

As the Supers headed back to campus, the rain stopped. "Look!" Katana said, pointing.

They all tilted their heads back. "What is that?" Harley turned on her camera. Bubbles the size of baseballs were floating down from the sky. When the sun's rays hit them, they looked like round rainbows. Supergirl popped one, and a flyer fell to the ground.

Katana read, "'In town for only twenty-four hours: the Krazy Karnival! You have only one day to experience the chills, thrills, and delights of the world's greatest and grandest amusement park!'"

As the Supers gathered the wayward flyers that littered the ground, a holographic billboard lit up the sky. A jolly man wearing a colorful hat trumpeted, "Come one, come all, to the new and improved Krazy Karnival! I'm J.J. Tetch, the new owner, and you're in for big surprises!"

"Surprises?" Harley said as her eyes twinkled. "No one loves surprises more than me!"

She immediately began broadcasting. "The world-famous Krazy Karnival is coming to Metropolis, and even if you can't be there . . . you can! That's because I'll be recording all the fun and all the **KRAZINESS** live on this channel!"

"It does sound like fun," Miss Martian said. Harley didn't even know she was there. "I wish I could go."

"Why can't you?" Harley asked.

"Crowds make me nervous," said Miss Martian. "I have trouble maneuvering through them."

"Stick with me," Harley generously offered. "I'm great at maneuvering. Plus, this is my chance to log the most viewers ever. I couldn't video the Junior Detectives sneaking up on Lion-Mane after I hit his foot. Or the great catch I made when he dropped the statue. Oh, sure, once he was in custody, I got it all on camera. But then, so did Lois Lane, who also had footage of the Supers leading the animals back. And that scene of a green monkey—Beast Boy—cradling a scared baby capuchin monkey and reuniting her with her mother. That was ratings gold for Lois!"

"It's not all about ratings, is it?" asked Miss Martian meekly.

"There's nothing wrong with big ratings," Harley said as she burst a bubble. "In fact, that's my goal: to have the most viewers in the world!"

Pied Piper was at the piano. He nodded to Cheetah, who was staring at the ground. As the teacher's fingers nimbly hit the piano keys, Cheetah raised her head. Harley watched her face transform. It was confident, yet vulnerable at the same time. Then that smile appeared. The famous Cheetah smile, as if she knew something you did not.

Cheetah winked at Harley and began to sing. It was a torch song—the heartfelt lyrics were about love and loss. As the last note hung in the air, the room was silent. Pied Piper leapt up. "Bravo, bravo!" he shouted. "I could feel that emotion. Beautiful. Seriously, beautiful. Thank you."

Cheetah took a bow, and when she swept past Harley, she said, "I would have won the Battle of the Bands. You should have a rematch."

In the front of the room, Cyborg had turned himself into a one-man band—a synthesizer with an electronic keyboard, and speakers coming out of his boots. As the rest of the class rocked to the beat, Harley kept thinking about her show. What could she do next to top it? Surely her viewers were expecting something spectacular. Was it enough to just live stream the Krazy Karnival?

"Harley?" Pied Piper called out. "You're up!"

Each student had been charged with doing a two-minute performance piece, whether it was singing solo or in a group, playing an instrument, or even karaoke.

"OH!" Harley cried. She hadn't prepared. "For my piece, I'm going to . . . to . . ." She looked around, desperate for inspiration. Suddenly, she saw it: Green Lantern was holding his tuba. "We're doing a duet!" she announced. As Harley dragged him to the front of the room, she whispered, "Just go along with me."

"What? No," Green Lantern protested, running his hand through his thick brown hair. "I'm doing a tuba solo—"

"*So low?*" Harley quipped, grabbing the tuba. "And how's about holding it *high* for a hat?"

When she placed the mouth of the tuba over her head, the class howled with laugher.

"Harley, please stop. Instruments are not toys," Pied Piper cautioned.

But Harley couldn't hear him from inside the tuba. "It's dark in here!" she cried out comically, getting more laughs from the classroom.

"Give that back to me," Green Lantern insisted. When he tried to wrench the tuba off Harley's head, it was stuck.

In a panic to un-tuba herself, Harley began running around the room, knocking over instruments and students. Green Lantern was in pursuit, causing even more calamity and chaos. Soon, Supers had taken sides, yelling, "Go, Harley!" and "Return the tuba!"

"Come back!" Green Lantern called out.

"This is epic!" Beast Boy cheered. "Harley, you're such a crack-up!"

"The class clown does it again," Cheetah said, yawning. "This is pathetic. She'll do anything for a laugh."

CHAPTER 15

"Hello, Harley!" Dr. Arkham was studying his desk through a magnifying glass. When he sat up, he was still holding it in front of his face. It made his left eye look huge. "I lost something," the school counselor explained. "But now I can't remember what it was."

"Was it this?" Harley asked, looking around. She grabbed a globe of Mars.

"Aha!" Arkham took the red planet from her. "Nope," he said, putting it down next to a tall stack of books, all written by him. "But I'll leave that here, in case I need to find it sometime."

Harley settled into her favorite chair. Arkham's office was dark and crowded with important-looking books, piles of paper, and an impressive stack of unopened mail. It smelled like the forest after the rain. Harley liked it in here. It was quiet—somber, even. She didn't feel the need to entertain when she was with Dr. Arkham.

"What's on your mind?" he asked. "Are you still feeling lonely and blue?"

"Blue, green, whatevs," Harley quipped. "What's not on my mind? You know me. Always thinking, thinking, thinking. Who knows what goes on in my noggin? It's so busy up there that sometimes I can't sleep." Harley paused. "Hey, doc, is it possible to think too much?"

As Arkham stroked his beard, she wondered why his head was bald when he had so much hair on his face.

"Hmm. Um. Yes. Sometimes we do tend to overthink," he said. "Tell me, what would you like to talk about today?"

"Aww, nothing," Harley said, jumping up and looking out the window. It was a sunny day and she could see Wonder Woman and Supergirl playing catch with a teacher's car. Harley turned back to the counselor. "It's just that some of my friends are pressuring me to spend more time with them."

"Go on," Arkham said.

"I would, but I'm busy, busy, busy. I've got my Harley's Quinntessentials to run, you know. It's a lot of work making people happy! Serious business, I tell ya. And it's not just on my Web channel. In person, too, I have to think of jokes and say funny stuff, and get all, you know . . . Harley-esque!"

"Go on," Arkham said.

"Whenever I see someone looking stressed, I want to cheer them up. So I'll tell a joke, or do a super-duper gymnastics move, or whatevs, even if I'm not feeling so great myself."

"Go on," Arkham said.

"I dunno," Harley said, slumping back into her chair. "Lots of kids call me the class clown, like that's a bad thing. And it makes me feel funny. Not ha-ha funny, but weird funny."

Arkham looked like he was asleep. But then he blinked his eyes open. "Harley," he said. "People underestimate the benefits of being happy. Laughter can make people feel better. You get that. Most don't."

"But what about hanging out with my friends? I would, but there's no time! Oh, wait," Harley said, interrupting herself. "I gotta cut today's session short. I'm busier than a bumblebee. There's someplace I gotta be."

"Harley!" Dr. Arkham called after her. "I need to ask you something."

"Yeah?"

He waved his magnifying glass in the air. "Why am I holding this?"

That afternoon in detention, Green Lantern refused even to look at Harley. "You could at least have warned me," Green Lantern griped. "We could have rehearsed."

"I didn't know until I saw the tuba," Harley admitted. "It was so big and shiny!"

"No talking!" Lucius Fox called out. Unlike Grodd, he did not appreciate detention duty.

"You have to admit, we had fun, right?" Harley whispered to Green Lantern. "Everyone was laughing."

"Shhh," Big Barda said.

Green Lantern gave Harley's question some thought. "Maybe a little, but it's not worth getting in trouble for."

"I dunno," Harley mused. "I kinda thought it was totally worth it. It sure cheered up the room!"

When Harley plopped her tray down on the table, Katana turned to her and said, "We were just talking about fan mail."

"I never get any," said Miss Martian, "unless you count the letters from my mom. She sends tons of them."

Katana sliced her veggie lasagna into perfectly square bite-sized pieces. "My parents email me twice a week," she noted. "Although I wouldn't call it fan mail. It's more like how-did-you-do-on-that-test mail."

"I hear from my grandmother all the time," Hawkgirl said. She was eating another helping of mac 'n' cheese 'n' mushrooms. "Half of it's fan mail, the other half is her worrying if I'm eating enough. Will someone take a photo of me with this?" She held up her plate and smiled at Batgirl.

Batgirl handed Hawkgirl's phone back and said, "I hear

from my dad constantly!" As if on cue, Commissioner Gordon waved to his daughter, then sat down at the faculty table. "Harley," Batgirl asked, "do your parents write to you?"

Harley poked holes in her chicken potpie. "Oh, they're so busy with their world travel, they don't have time to write," she said.

"What do they do?" asked Big Barda.

"Tightrope walkers," Harley said quickly. "All around the world, everywhere there are tightropes."

Hawkgirl sent the photo Batgirl had taken of her to her grandmother, then said, "Harley, I thought you told me your parents were accountants."

"Did I say that?" Harley asked. "Well, they used to be. Now they're librarians."

Batgirl perked up. "I didn't know that!"

"Oh, sure, they have a library in their motor home, and they only have cookbooks, because they used to be professional chefs."

"So they're tightrope-walking accountant librarian chefs?" asked Barda.

"They were chefs and accountants, but that was after they sold spaceship insurance," Harley said, not meeting anyone's gaze.

"Wait!" Beast Boy leaned over from the next table. "You told me you were raised by raccoons!"

Harley laughed. "Did I say that? My bad. I meant coyotes."

"You must get tons of fan mail because of your Web channel," Miss Martian said. "Tell us about it!"

Harley was glad to change the subject. She tried to look modest. It was true. She probably got more fan mail than the others did. In fact, she was always telling her viewers to "Let me know!" And they did.

"I answer all my fan mail right away," Wonder Woman was saying.

"I save them up and answer once a week," Supergirl said. "I noticed I get more emails after a battle or Save the Day."

"I don't get as much as the two of you," Bumblebee offered. "But I love it when fans send me honey. There's this group who calls themselves the Bumblebee Honeys, and they're my unofficial fan club. I always send them a handwritten thank-you note when they send honey. Anyone get anything interesting recently?"

"I just got this," Harley said, pulling a mirror out of her pocket.

The girls gathered around. A round of "oohs" went up in the air as they admired the gorgeous hand mirror.

"That's carved from teak," Katana said, inspecting the craftsmanship. "Look at the inlaid pearl."

"It looks old," noted Supergirl. "Like a family heirloom."

Bumblebee held it up to the light. "Wow, my reflection looks like I'm actually in the mirror, like it's three-D."

Harley took it back and peered at herself. She wiggled her

ears. "**WOWZA!**" she exclaimed. "You're right. I look more real in the mirror than I do right here!"

"Who sent it?" Supergirl asked.

Harley shrugged. "Don't know."

No one was surprised by this. School packages were often delivered by drones or birds, or on the backs of rockets.

"There was no name or return address on it," Harley continued. "But the note said: 'To Harley Quinn, from your biggest fan.'"

For the next few days, Harley was never without the mirror. She used it when she needed to fix her hair, or after eating. "No one wants to see a close-up of a Super with food in their teeth, am I right?" she asked. Harley even used it to practice her lines for her Web channel.

"Harley, please put your mirror away," Pied Piper said. "I'd like you to focus on what I'm about to show you." He began playing a video of singers from around the world doing their interpretation of the same song. "Focus, Harley. Focus."

Easy for him to say, she thought as she tucked the mirror back in her pocket. She looked up. Now, what was that she was supposed to do?

Back in her room, Harley took the hand mirror out again. "Hello, HQ fans," she said as she watched herself. "Harley here, asking, How would you like a super-duper exclusive behind-the-scenes Harley-riffic special at Krazy Karnival?"

She was pleased with her idea. It was sure to attract attention. After all, everyone had heard of Krazy Karnival. So why not turn the amusement park's twenty-four hours in Metropolis into a mega-special, Harley-style?

"Let me know," Harley practiced saying. "Send me a message!" She was about to put the mirror down, but stopped and gasped.

It looked like the Harley in the mirror winked at her.

It was impossible to get hold of Jervis "J.J." Tetch, the Krazy Karnival's new owner. Not even Batgirl could find him, and if she couldn't, then no one could.

"He's elusive, that's for sure," Batgirl said as Harley leaned over her shoulder and tapped the computer screen. "Um, Harley, personal space, remember?"

Harley stepped back.

From what Lois reported, Harley knew that J.J. had recently taken over the amusement park, but he was something of a mystery man.

"Maybe I should do this later," Batgirl said as Harley did

a tumbling routine and nailed her landing a few inches from Batgirl's workshop area.

There were lots of sharp tools and confusing gadgets and wires and whatnots. Harley opened a black velvet box and examined a teeny-tiny silver pellet nestled beside a ring.

"No, no, no! Search for Tetch now. I'll be quiet," promised Harley as she held the pellet to the light.

Batgirl let out a huge sigh. She sighed a lot around Harley. "Careful with that. Remember when you put a micro-camera on Bumblebee?" Harley nodded. "Well, that gave me an idea, and you're holding it."

"What is it?" Harley asked, squinting at the object.

"I've been toying with the prototype of a micro ring-activated drone camera," Batgirl said, taking the pellet from Harley. "I'm calling it the QuinnCam."

Harley beamed. It was named after her! She slipped her mirror out of her pocket and said into her reflection, "Harley Quinn here, reporting live via the QuinnCam!"

The bubbles started slowly, drifting down from the clouds like a summer's rain. Only instead of showers, it felt like happiness blanketing Metropolis. Supergirl spotted them first as she flew back to school, having spent the night at her Aunt Martha and Uncle Jonathan's farm.

"The Krazy Karnival has arrived!" Supergirl announced as she flew around the dorm, throwing cookies to everyone she passed. Aunt Martha always made enough for the entire school.

Harley reached for her mallet and camera. As an afterthought, she tucked the velvet box from Batgirl's workshop into her pocket, just in case. "It's showtime!" she announced, looking in her hand mirror. "Miss Martian, let's go!"

For days Harley had been publicizing it: "Coming soon, the Krazy Karnival on Harley's Quinntessentials, streaming live!" And in what she claimed was a spur-of-the-moment genius idea, she promised, "Music fans, get this! We're gonna have a rematch of the HQ Battle of the Bands at the Krazy Karnival! So tune in to see who the winner will be!"

She hoped J.J. Tetch would be as enthusiastic as she was. Should she have gotten his permission first? Harley brushed away her doubts. Better to do first and ask later, she reminded herself. "Right, Miss Martian?" she said as she pushed past the crowds toward the sights and sounds of the Krazy Karnival.

"Huh?" the mind reader asked.

"Are you reading my mind now?" Harley said.

"Um, no," Miss Martian protested. "Mind-reading is my superpower. I only use it when I have to, for the good of the world or to save lives."

Harley laughed. "There's so much going on in my mind, I doubt you could read it anyway. Try!"

"I don't think so," Miss Martian demurred.

"No, go ahead," Harley insisted. "You have my permission."

"Okay," Miss Martian said, closing her eyes. After a couple of seconds, she said, "It's confusing, that's for sure!"

Harley grinned proudly.

Near the entrance was a long line. It looked like the entire population of Metropolis was in attendance, in addition to most of nearby Gotham City, and every place in between. Schools from every country and galaxy were represented, since students got in free. And, of course, everyone from Super Hero High was there, except for the teachers and Principal Waller, who were at an Excellence in Education Conference on Upsilon Andromedae B—the planet, not the band.

Harley was in heaven.

"We are going to have the best day ever!" she enthused.

"I'm not sure," Miss Martian said, looking at the crowds. She started to fade. "There are so many people here."

"Exactly!" said Harley. "You read my mind! The more the merrier, and the merrier the more viewers, and the more viewers the more popular Harley's Quinntessentials! What are we waiting for? Let the adventure begin!"

CHAPTER 16

"Excuse me, pardon me, excuse me, Harley Quinn here, and I need to be there!" she said, pointing.

The giant bubble machine rose from the center of the carnival looking like a colossal jukebox with a rainbow of bubbles shooting out as music played. As Harley made her way past the crowd of excited guests, Miss Martian trailed along, looking at the video screens that were everywhere. On them, J.J. Tetch was touting, "You're in for the time of your life!"

"Hurry!" Harley called out. She wasn't sure if her friend was way behind or had turned invisible again. "Stick with me, Miss Martian, and you'll have a day you'll never forget," Harley promised. "You can help me put up my cameras all over the place. The more the better!"

"Maybe I'll just go back to school," Miss Martian said, out of breath. "I have a good book I'm in the middle of. It's called *The Shout of the Clam*."

"Look! It's the Green Team! Helloooo, Green Team," Harley said, waving. The teens shouted and waved back.

"Did you get permission yet?" Miss Martian asked as Harley hurried her along, placing cameras along the way. "To do a behind-the-scenes here and to host the Battle of the Bands?" She saw band members lugging their instruments.

Harley snorted. "You sound like Hawkgirl."

Miss Martian smiled shyly. "Thank you."

"Not yet. Let's find the owner of the Karnival. He's gotta say yes to an interview! He'd be crazy not to. And as for the Battle of the Bands, I think it's totally necessary, don't you?"

"But where will it be? When will it be? You just told the bands to show up, and . . . and—"

Harley stopped and shook her head. "Miss Martian, there's nothin' to worry about. We'll figure it out when we get there! That's the Harley way."

Miss Martian's eyes widened with concern, but she clamped her mouth shut.

At the gates, cheerful carnival workers decked out in colorful light-up costumes handed out treats, like Raspberry Sugar Bombs that made hilarious exploding noises when you bit down and Cotton Candy Clouds so light that if you didn't eat them immediately, they floated away. Some students from Metropolis Elementary were carrying deep-fried hot dogs on sticks, while others ate gooey slices of pizza. Busloads of kids were screaming and laughing. Though they had just arrived, their chaperones already looked exhausted as they grabbed for the free light-up necklaces and "Krazy" hats as fast as the carnival workers could pass them out.

Bumblebee flew up to Harley and Miss Martian. "Isn't this great?" she asked. "I'm going to get one of those hats with lace and sparkles. What about you two?"

"No time for hats," Harley said. "We can't wait to get to the fun, isn't that right, Miss Martian?"

"Oh, well, a hat might be nice," Miss Martian said softly. Just then, a carnival worker with white wings and silver hair plopped a flowerpot hat on Miss Martian's head, much to her delight.

"It looks lovely on you!" the worker said. "I'm Silver Swan, and I must say, the peach and yellow flatter your green skin."

Miss Martian blushed again.

"Here's one for you," a muscled man in yellow said to Harley. He was holding a jester's hat. Four colorful padded points that resembled donkey ears in red, green, purple, and yellow flopped merrily. Their tips were weighed down with jingly bells. But before he could put it on her, Harley started running.

"Look!" she cried, dragging Bumblebee as Miss Martian hurried to keep up. "Over there!"

Bumblebee rode the Honeycomb Hideaway ride again and again. It was a delight to sit in the golden honeycomb cups as they sailed in and out of honeycomb-land, bees buzzing around in sweet harmony. The attraction's song was the kind that played over and over in your head, long after the ride was over. "Bees, bees, a world of bees . . ."

Meanwhile, Harley and Miss Martian were mesmerized by the wonderland of lights and sounds and tech. Everything was so retro that it was daringly modern. Old carnival attractions had been expanded and improved and were awash in neon colors. Everywhere you looked there were digital displays controlling the overhead aerial holograms of jolly J.J. reminding everyone, "As my guest at Krazy Karnival, it's your job to have fun!"

Harley entered the Game Zone. Her heart was racing. So much to see and do!

"Step right up! Test your strength! Who will show 'em how it's done?" The burly carnival worker wearing a teeny top hat was holding up a sledgehammer. "Ring the bell and win a prize! Who will be next? How about you, girlie? Think you're strong enough to ring the bell?"

Harley looked at the shiny bell at the top of the Strength Test. "Hit this target down here," the carnival worker explained. "And the puck goes up. If you're strong enough and it goes high enough, it hits the bell and you win a prize!"

That was all that Harley had to hear. "I'm game!" she

shouted, twirling her mallet in one hand. "And I don't need your sledgehammer. I brought something of my own."

Setting up her camera to make sure this was streaming live, Harley got in position. She gripped her mallet tight and focused on the target. Then, with all her might, she brought her mallet down hard.

Cheers rose all around. The worker's jaw hung open. Harley had hit the target so hard that the puck broke through the Strength Test game and sent the bell sailing into the air.

"There's my prize!" Harley announced, catching the solid metal bell before it hit the ground. "I'm keeping this!"

Harley bowed to the cheering crowd as she walked on. She could not believe how much fun everyone was having. It was as if they were in a haze of happiness. She hooted to Cheetah and Star Sapphire, who were wearing fetching hats (a beret for Cheetah, a crown for Sapphire) and taking selfies. Both smiled warmly at Harley and hooted back.

"I'm getting a headache," Miss Martian said softly. She adjusted her flowerpot hat.

By then, Bumblebee had left them to join Katana and Big Barda on the Rock 'n' Roller Coaster—where you sat in faux boulders as they plummeted down a mountain. Also on the ride were several members of the Korugar Academy marching band. Every time the roller coaster went around a bend or dove down, instead of screaming they played their instruments as loudly as possible.

"This isn't helping my headache," Miss Martian whimpered.

"Too much fun can do that to you, if you're not used to it," Harley explained. "I never get headaches."

"I think I need to sit down," Miss Martian said. She looked wobbly. "You go ahead. I'll catch up later."

The Green Team made their way past, all holding up ice cream cones as if they were Olympic torches.

"Okay," Harley said to Miss Martian. "See you in a bit. I'm off to find J.J."

He had to be somewhere, right? After all, this was his carnival. Harley knew what he looked like. The roundish face. The wide smile. The twinkling eyes. And that hat! That outlandish top hat with sparkles and lights on it. How could you miss someone who looks like that?

As Harley made her way past Katana and Frost holding hands and running under a shower of flower petals in the Orchid Zone, she paused. It was so cool that Supers who normally didn't hang out together were having fun here.

That was when she saw him. The elusive Jervis "J.J." Tetch. Only, someone else was about to interview him first!

The reporter was just getting into position. She had

checked her notes and made sure the microphone was on. But before she could say, "Lois Lane here with Jervis 'J.J.'—" she was blindsided by a flurry of red and blue and black and white hurdling toward her.

"Harley?" Lois said, just before she ducked.

Harley had leapt over her and was now standing right next to the new owner of Krazy Karnival. With her back to Lois, Harley launched right into her interview.

"Hi, J.J. Tetch. You don't mind if I call you J.J., do you, J.J.?" Harley asked. "I'm—"

"Everyone knows who you are," said J.J. He was all smiles. "You're Harley Quinn of Harley's Quinntessentials. I'm your biggest fan!"

"I am? Um . . . you are?" she asked. "So nice of you! Hey, how about an exclusive interview? My fans wanna hear all about this Krazy Karnival of yours!"

He looked over at Lois, who shrugged as if to say, "Go ahead."

"Well, all right," J.J. said, handing Harley a jumbo whirly-swirly rainbow lollipop. "Anything for you, Miss Quinn."

Harley was beaming. This J.J. fellow was the nicest, smartest person in the world, she decided. "So, J.J.," she began, "can you tell my maybe millions and zillions of viewers why you bought this famous amusement park?"

He straightened his massive hat, which had a habit of tilting to the right. "My goal is to bring happiness and fun to the world," he said. Harley nodded so much holding her camera that it looked like he was jumping up and down. "The Krazy Karnival was up for sale—the last owner, who ran it for fifty years, decided to retire. So I bought it!"

There was a crowd gathered behind them, waving to the camera.

"Tell us more," Harley urged.

"Well, this is the best Krazy Karnival ever," J.J. boasted with a sweep of his hand. His cheeks flushed red with delight. "It's got new rides as well as hip and healthy new foods, with some new twists on old favorites," he added, "like corn on the cob that pops into popcorn, and funny funnel cakes!"

"Funny funnel cakes?" Harley enthused as they started walking. "I love funny, and I love funnel cakes!"

Just then a group of teens wandered past. "Hey! Hey!" J.J. called out. "It's the famous Green Team, thrill-seekers and adventurers. I was hoping you'd be here. We made special hats just for you," he said cheerfully. He motioned to some of his workers, who promptly hauled a box of hats over to the carnival owner. "Try them on for size!"

As the Green Team put on their green-and-black bowler hats, Harley whispered to the camera, "So far it's been all talk, but now—fingers crossed—maybe J.J. will give us a behind-the-scenes tour. . . ."

"Have fun, Green Team," J.J. was saying as he waved goodbye to them. He turned to Harley. "How about a tour?"

Harley winked at the camera. "It's like he was reading my mind!" she exclaimed.

Just as J.J. took the lead, he stopped to adjust Captain Cold's pirate hat. "That's better. This really suits you."

"Thanks," Captain Cold said, offering him a smile that was uncharacteristically warm and pleasant. The rest of his Cap'n Cold and Crew heavy metal band giggled. "Nice amusement park you have here, Mr. Tetch, sir," Captain Cold continued. "I love it! And, Harley, we adore your Web channel! Can't wait for the Battle of the Bands. Krazy Karnival is the perfect place for it. I want to wish everyone good luck!"

"You heard that right here," Harley said to the camera. "Even Captain Cold loves Harley's Quinntessentials, and he's not the easiest person on the planet to please!"

"You're hosting a Battle of the Bands here?" J.J. asked, looking pleased. "At my modest little amusement park? I'm honored!"

"**WOWZA, YOWZA,** I thought you'd like that," Harley said to J.J. She watched as the gang from CAD Academy went their way, whistling and waving to those they passed, then noted: "Captain Cold sure is in a good mood. I've never seen him like that before."

"Oh, Harley, my dear," J.J. said. His eyes were moist. "You don't get it, do you?"

"Get what?" They passed another towering Sweet Treats stand, and he handed her an edible candy cup filled with the most delicious double-dipped chocolate berries she had ever tasted.

"It's you who people love. He was responding to your effervescence. It's why the masses tune in to your Web channel. To see you, Miss Quinn. They love you!"

Harley felt her face flush. She wondered if he was right. Was everyone watching her? Everyone at home? Everyone at school? A lot of times she'd have a really awesome segment, but Wonder Woman or some of the others would miss it.

"Sorry, Harley, I was doing homework," Batgirl would say.

"Did I miss a segment?" Poison Ivy would ask. "Chompy needed attention."

"Harley, you're always on, and I got stuff I gotta do," Beast Boy would tell her. "But I'll try to catch up."

"They love me?" Harley repeated. "Aww, J.J., you're such a joker. But if you want to say it again, Harley's not gonna stop you!"

He laughed good-naturedly. "Harley, I've got a great idea that could benefit us both! But first, I have some business to attend to. I'll give you an exclusive interview shortly, but in the meantime, why don't we get you one of my famous Krazy Karnival hats?" He looked around. His carnival workers were everywhere. Harley thought some of them looked familiar. "M.M.!" he called. "A hat for Ms. Quinn. You must have missed her when she came in!"

"So sorry, sir!" the muscled man in the yellow costume

with a green mask said. "I'll make sure Harley Quinn gets a hat!"

As he hurried away, J.J. ran after him. "Wait up!" he cried. "Not just any hat. I want to make sure Ms. Quinn gets one of our super-special ones!"

Harley beamed. This was fun, fun, fun!

CHAPTER 17

As fun as it would be to have her own super-special hat, Harley didn't have the patience to wait around. There were rides to go on, and games to play, and treats to eat, and . . . and . . . As she raced past the Ukulele United band cheering each other on at the Wheeeee Skeeeeeball game, Harley pivoted and doubled back. Something green had caught her eye.

"Why are you just sitting there?" she asked a glum Miss Martian.

Nearby, Batgirl was at the Magic Donut Maker, watching eagerly as it shot free fresh hot mini-doughnuts into the crowd. "Me next! Me next!" Batgirl called out, jumping up and down, waving both hands.

Miss Martian closed her eyes and brought her fingertips to her temple. "My headache is getting worse," she said. One of the flowers on her hat was drooping over the front of her face. "Maybe I should just go back to the dorm and take a nap."

"And miss all the fun?" Harley asked. "You don't want to do that."

Miss Martian shook her head. "I do want to stay, but this headache is crushing me."

"Maybe you should look for Poison Ivy," Harley suggested. "She always knows what to do when someone is feeling a little blue. And your face is all blue right now. Here, look." She held out her hand mirror.

"Can you stay with me?" Miss Martian asked. She didn't like what she saw in the mirror. "I don't feel like being alone right now. This place is too crowded."

"But if it's crowded, you aren't alone," Harley reasoned.

"Never mind," Miss Martian said. Harley could see her disappearing as she began to walk away.

"Miss Martian, wait!" Harley called after her. Even though she didn't want to miss a minute of fun, her friend needed her. "Let's look for Ivy together."

"Have you seen Poison Ivy?" Harley asked Bumblebee. She paused. "You and Miss Martian are supposed to be having a great time like everyone else, but instead you're acting like worrywarts!"

"I'm getting a strange feeling about this place," Bumblebee said. All the flowers on Miss Martian's hat wilted, making it look like it was melting. "Um, maybe you should ditch the hat," she suggested.

Miss Martian reached up. "But I love this hat. It was a gift."

Harley studied the hat. "It's looking goopy, which is kinda Krazy-awesome!"

Reluctantly, Miss Martian took off her hat. She took a deep cleansing breath. "I'm starting to feel better already," she said, surprised.

Bumblebee lowered her voice. "Have you two noticed how weird everyone is acting?"

"Weird? No," said Harley. "It's Krazy Karnival time, and everyone's in a great mood."

"Yeah, and what about those kids from CAD Academy?" Bumblebee said.

"What about them? Captain Cold's been really nice," Harley pointed out.

"Exactly!" said Bumblebee. "When have you ever known him to be nice?"

Harley hesitated. "Uh, never?" Then she lit up. "That's the power of the Krazy Karnival!"

Just then a familiar group of teens brushed past. "Hey, Green Team?" Harley yelled. "Where are you going? You're heading the wrong way. That's the exit!"

They all stared straight ahead as they kept walking.

Lois Lane raced after them as they left the amusement park. "How about an interview?" she asked.

"Um, Harley?" Miss Martian said, tapping her on the shoulder. "Harley? Um, Harley, look!"

Harley followed Miss Martian's gaze. Bumblebee was staring at the same thing. Harley whipped out her camera. "It's a Harley's Quinntessentials exclusive!" she cried. She aimed the camera toward the sky, unable to believe what was happening.

Everyone was gawking with their heads tilted up. Everyone but Bumblebee, who was now flying around warning people: "Something is wrong, something is very wrong!"

"Nothing's wrong," Beast Boy said, smiling. "Everything's great!"

"Yes, everything is lovely," Cheetah insisted as she adjusted her beret.

"She's right," said Katana. "Cheetah's right again!"

"Look!" Bumblebee cried, pointing at the Bubble Machine.

"Whatever is happening, you're seeing it here first!" Harley told her viewers. "And so is the rest of the world, because we're broadcasting live on Harley's Quinntessentials!"

"This is not good," Miss Martian warned.

"It's not good, it's *great!*" said The Flash.

The others agreed. All around, Krazy Karnival guests were watching the High-Tetch Bubble Machine. Small bubbles had given way to one gigantic bubble . . . and it kept getting bigger and bigger.

"So pretty," said Frost, sighing.

Ratcatcher was crying and didn't care who saw him. "The beauty of it!" he said as Captain Cold nodded in agreement.

Bumblebee and Miss Martian glanced at each other as Harley kept her camera on. "Viewers, I'm not sure what we're seeing here at Krazy Karnival," she reported, "but it's crazy, all right, and I'm certain the carnival's breaking a new world record for the biggest bubble."

By now it was covering the entire Krazy Karnival, and closing up to encase it—making it look like everyone was inside a giant dome. The bigger it got, the happier everyone was. When it sealed shut, all the guests started cheering and clapping.

"No, no!" Bumblebee shouted. "Don't you see? We're trapped in here!"

"I've got the exclusive," Harley proclaimed. "That's right, world, something weird is going on at Krazy Karnival, and to find out what it is, stay tuned right here on Harley's Quinntessentials!"

Miss Martian shook her head. "This is bad. Really bad," she said before turning invisible.

CHAPTER 18

"No!" Bumblebee shouted. But no one paid attention to her. "No, something's wrong."

Amused, Harley recorded her using her blasters to try to penetrate the bubble. "We're trapped!" Bumblebee cried. "The bubble has created a barrier to the outside world."

Harley tossed her mallet up high into the air. It made a *klunk* when it hit the bubble. "It's totally solid!" she said admiringly.

"It's not right," Miss Martian said, barely audible. Harley could hardly see her. "And neither is anyone here. They're not themselves!"

"We're happy here!" said Hawkgirl as she twirled past them with her arms out to her sides. She was wearing a colorful Viking helmet. "Why break the bubble when we can stay and have fun?"

"That's right," Thunder and Lightning chimed in as they executed silly synchronized-swim moves to imaginary music.

Their fluffy cloud-shaped hats looked the same, but on closer inspection, one was cirrus and one was cumulus. "There's no better place to be than at Krazy Karnival right now," the sisters said in unison.

"I totally agree with that," Batgirl said, adjusting the rainbow-colored mortarboard on her head.

"Hey, can you guys help me try to break this bubble?" Bumblebee asked.

"Whatever for?" said Wonder Woman. She was wearing an oversized bonnet festooned with feathers. "It looks so cool!"

"'Cause it will be fun to try?" Bumblebee said.

"Fun!" shouted Wonder Woman. "I'm up for that. I love fun!"

But when Wonder Woman tried to break the bubble, she couldn't. Nor could Supergirl, or Cyborg, or anyone else— though it didn't look like they were trying very hard. In fact, it looked like they were goofing off.

"It's totally solid!" Harley reported. "I guess we'll just have to stay and have fun!" Adding, "Reporting live from inside the bubble."

"I've got a bad feeling about this," Bumblebee kept saying.

Miss Martian, barely visible, nodded. The carnival workers were now leaving their posts. Rides went unattended. Some attractions, like the Tilt-a-Whirl, were spinning faster and faster, to the delight of the riders. Guests helped themselves to the food carts, and others were grabbing armfuls of prizes in the Game Zone.

"Excuse me. Um, excuse me?" Miss Martian said to Silver Swan. "Should you really be leaving the Tunnel of Love when there are still people inside? You work there, right?"

Silver Swan adjusted the feathered crown on her head and flapped her wings. "I'm on my break," she replied. "No one tells me what to do. Well, almost no one . . ."

"But it's dark in the Tunnel of Love and it might not be safe. What if the ride goes off the rails?" Miss Martian asked.

"We'll have to deal with that when it happens, then, won't we?" Silver Swan winked at her before flying off to join Cupid, who was abandoning her post at the Slings and Arrows game.

Miss Martian was speechless as chaos began to consume the amusement park.

"This is so exciting," Harley said, swinging her camera left and right, up and down, to get all the angles. She was glad they had placed cameras everywhere, and cut to other scenes using her remote video control board.

"Slow down. I'm trying to—" Miss Martian pleaded. "I can't read anyone's mind. Please slow down!"

Harley stopped. "Wait," she said, as if hit by a wayward thought. "I thought you only read minds if you thought lives might be in danger."

CHAPTER 19

"I don't know what's happening," Miss Martian said. "But whatever it is, it's not normal. Look!"

Harley swung around to see Cyborg and Big Barda scrambling up the side of the Ferris wheel while it was still moving. The massive steel structure was several stories high and circling nonstop.

"Look at me!" Cyborg yelled as he hung off one of the passenger cars hundreds of feet in the air.

"That looks like fun!" Barda shouted. "Wait for me!"

Harley gasped as Barda leapt from one of the moving passenger cars to another. "We're loopy!" she shouted as the Ferris wheel continued to spin.

"Faster, faster!" Cyborg urged Supergirl, who was in the air twirling the ride as if it were a pinwheel.

The kids in the passenger cars were squealing with joy.

Suddenly, something cold hit Harley in the head. "Hey!" she yelled, expecting to see Captain Cold or Frost. Instead,

Mandy Bowin was standing behind her holding an empty ice cream cone.

"Oops!" Mandy said, giggling. "Sorry!" she yelled as she ran away and joined Hawkgirl, who handed her another cone and said, "Okay, now this time hit Cheetah!"

Harley laughed as she followed them toward an unsuspecting Cheetah. This was sure to be a classic for her "Super Hero Goofs and Giggles" segment. On her way, Harley passed Batgirl stuffing her face with fried candy bars. Batgirl had even stockpiled a bunch of them on top of her hat and was balancing them as she strode purposefully back toward the Magic Donut Maker.

"Hey, Batgirl," Harley called out. "How many viewers are watching right now?"

Batgirl wobbled as she came to a stop, continuing to balance her sugary load. "Wait, look at this!" she said. Her hat almost fell off, but she pulled it on tighter. Everyone gathered around as Batgirl projected the screen into the air from her Bat-phone.

"This is Lois Lane reporting live from downtown Metropolis," she was saying. "Multiple robberies are happening all over the city. There would probably be even more if there weren't so many citizens at the Krazy Karnival. As for the perpetrators, all evidence points to the Green Team, a group of teens wearing green bowler hats. No one is safe with them on the loose," Lois continued. "Commissioner

Gordon and his police have been called in and are doing all they can. However, they could really use the help of the super heroes from Super Hero High!"

"We're trapped!" shouted Miss Martian from inside the bubble. "We're trapped!"

"It's weird, but the only signal that can get out of the bubble is your show, Harley," Batgirl said, trying to stifle a giggle. "No phones, no messages. Nothing." Harley gave her a sideways look. Batgirl was not known to be a giggler. Something strange was definitely going on. "And the only information that can come in to us is Lois Lane's Web channel!" Batgirl said before laughing so hard she was in tears.

Lois was still talking. "It appears the super heroes are all in attendance at the Krazy Karnival. Wait, what's that?" Lois's voice remained calm, but her eyes widened. "I can't believe what I'm seeing. It looks like the Green Team is . . . Can it be? The Green Team is multiplying!"

"The Green Team's doing math?" Harley quipped.

"There are reports that though they started out as a dozen, there are now one hundred members fanning out into every corner of Metropolis!" said Lois.

"*WOWZA!* They're multiplying themselves! *DOUBLE WOWZA!* Triple, even!" Harley cried as the magnitude of what was happening finally hit her.

"It's worse than you think," Batgirl said, doubling over

with laughter. "The joke's on you!"

Harley could not believe her eyes. Or her ears. Batgirl had reprogrammed the video screens that were dotted around the amusement park. Now, instead of J.J. reminding everyone to have a great day, it was broadcasting Harley's Quinntessentials, where "Harley" was reporting from the Krazy Karnival.

"Lalala . . . The Supers of Super Hero High don't care about what's happening in Metropolis!" a fake video Harley said. "We just want to have fun!"

"What's that?" Bumblebee said, flying over to Batgirl.

"THAT'S NOT ME!" Harley shouted. She could not take her eyes off her image on the screen. "I'm standing right here!"

But it sure did look like her. "It's showtime!" the Harley look-alike said. "Sure, the Green Team may be taking over Metropolis, but we have more important stuff to do, like go on rides and play games!"

Batgirl switched back to Lois Lane's Web channel. "Has Harley Quinn gone crazy?" Lois was asking. "What's up with our beloved super heroes when we need them most?"

Batgirl punched in some numbers. "No one is paying attention to Lois, or any other channel, Harley. They're all tuned in to you. Yay! You rule!"

"THAT'S NOT ME!" Harley shouted.

"It sure looks like you," noted Bumblebee. "Look, that Harley even has the same little freckles you have."

Harley pulled out her hand mirror and did a freckle check. They were still there. "I need to get on the air right now and fix this," she said as she squinted at her fake self.

"Hello, Harley Quinn here," Harley said to the camera. "I'm here to tell you that there's a fake Harley out there—"

Her broadcast was interrupted by the Fake Harley. "And I'm here to tell you that it's me, Harley, who's being fake and funny!"

"No, that's not me," Real Harley insisted before being interrupted again. The video screens jumped back and forth between Harleys.

"Loyal viewers, come along for the ride as we watch the Supers act really strange!" Fake Harley said. "What will happen? Stay tuned to find out."

Suddenly footage of more Supers acting out in general mayhem and chaos and of rides going haywire were blasting on the screen.

"I—I don't know what's happening," Harley sputtered. "I'm not in control here!"

"Then who is?" Batgirl asked seriously, and burst out laughing.

The real Harley was running in circles to calm herself. Miss Martian made sure to be very, very still so as not to get caught in her whirlwind. Meanwhile, Bumblebee was buzzing around the amusement park, getting a fix on what was happening.

"Wow, she's not herself," Bumblebee whispered to Miss Martian as they watched Batgirl reprogram the Magic Donut Maker. It began to pump out so many doughnuts that they seemed to be raining down over everyone in the vicinity.

"No one is," noted Miss Martian. "Well, you, me, and Harley, but it's like everyone else here is acting like someone other than themselves."

"Yeah, it's like something's happened to everyone," said Bumblebee. "But what?"

"I had a huge headache when I first got here," Miss Martian said. "It hurt so much, and it wasn't until I took off my . . . hat. Hat! It's the hats!"

"Ooookay . . . ," Bumblebee said slowly. "Now *you're* acting weird."

"No! It is the hats," Miss Martian insisted. "They are affecting everyone's minds. You, me, and Harley . . . no hats. Batgirl, Supergirl, Cheetah? The Green Team? They are all wearing the hats."

Bumblebee looked around. Batgirl was now doing a doughnut dance she had just invented, and Cheetah was wandering around passing out compliments to everyone she came across.

"You're right," Bumblebee said. "They're all wearing hats and not acting like themselves."

Harley sat on the ground and moaned. "And the person who is most not like herself is ME. With THAT one on the air." She pointed to a video screen where the fake Harley was telling everyone to "get reckless and wild!"

"It is the hats," Miss Martian repeated. "We have to get them."

Harley nodded slowly. "Okay." She pointed to Batgirl. "Let's start with hers."

Batgirl was sitting on the ground stuffing more doughnuts into her mouth when Bumblebee shouted, "Three, two, one . . . go!"

The three rushed Batgirl. "Hey!" she cried. "What's going on?"

"Give us your hat!" Harley yelled.

"No way!" Batgirl said, pulling it tighter on her head.

"Please," said Miss Martian. "It is harming you."

"Is not!" said Batgirl. She scaled up the tall skywalk that circled the Krazy Karnival and was now hanging upside-down with her legs bent over a rail. She held her hat on her head with one hand and finished a doughnut with the other.

Bumblebee flew up to her. "I'll explain later," she said, attempting a fly-by to snatch the hat from Batgirl's head.

Immediately, Batgirl reached for her Batarang and flung it

at Bumblebee, who ducked out of the way.

"Hey!" yelled Bumblebee. "You almost hit me!"

"No one touches my hat!" Batgirl grumbled.

"She's not herself," Miss Martian reminded Bumblebee. "We need to get her hat and destroy it to be sure she won't put it back on!"

Harley leapt onto the nearby Gravitron ride. She used its spinning centrifugal force to propel her up and landed atop the metal mesh roof of the skywalk. From there, Harley looked down at Batgirl, who was still hanging upside down, enjoying the view and the snacks.

In one move, Harley grabbed Batgirl's hat and tossed it up toward Bumblebee, who hit it with her blasters. But in her hurry, Harley lost her grip. She began to free-fall toward the ground.

"HELP!" Harley yelled, flailing her arms and kicking. "Someone catch me!"

Before Bumblebee could get to her, Batgirl swooped in on a thin wire and grabbed Harley. They both landed lightly on the ground.

"Thanks, Batgirl," Harley said as she smoothed out her shirt.

"What just happened?" Batgirl asked. "I feel sort of weird."

"Too many doughnuts," Harley quipped. "Come on, we'll explain. But first we have to make a plan."

"It's fun and chaos here inside the bubble," Fake Harley was reporting. On the screen was video of the Supers trying to tear the hats off the heads of the others. "Like a game of capture the flag, my fellow super heroes are playing Grab the Hat. Never before have more people been more in love with their hats," she said, laughing. "What's more important than hats? Nothing!"

The footage was strangely compelling. Viewers had never seen anything like it. Some Supers, like The Flash, were too fast for just one super hero to catch. Katana and Big Barda were fighting over Barda's purple hat with red feathers, even though Katana had a jaunty green Robin Hood—style hat of her own. "Mine!" Barda shouted. Everyone, friends and enemies, was engaged in fights over hats. As the mess grew, so did the number of viewers of Harley's Quinntessentials.

"Every news channel in the world has locked into HQ, but it looks like Fake Harley is still overriding your real reports," Batgirl said as she looked at her chart. She was keeping track of which Supers had had their hats confiscated and which ones were still wearing theirs.

"What about Lois Lane's reports?" Harley asked.

Batgirl shook her head. "No one's watching that, even with Metropolis under siege. They'd rather watch you."

Separating super heroes from their hats proved difficult.

"No one's getting this hat!" Supergirl yelled as she flew toward the top of the bubble. Wonder Woman, Hawkgirl, and Bumblebee were in pursuit.

"It's controlling you!" Bumblebee said.

"It is not, and you are starting to bug me!" Supergirl called out as she hovered out of reach. "I love my hat! It makes me happy! Plus, it's *so* cute."

"It *is* cute," Wonder Woman said as she flung herself against the thick wall of the bubble. "But there's nothing cute about mind control, and that bonnet you're wearing is making you all wonky. I wasn't myself until Batgirl Bataranged mine off my head!"

"Wonky?" Supergirl said. "Who are you calling wonky?" For a moment, Bumblebee distracted her with a sonic blast. In that second, Wonder Woman swooped in and got the hat, tossing it to Catwoman, who used her whip to destroy it.

Bumblebee gave her a thumbs-up. One more hat destroyed, one more Super to help get rid of the hats. What started out difficult was getting easier. Or was it? Harley wasn't sure. There were still hundreds and hundreds of guests to contend with, and they were totally out of control. So much was happening, Harley didn't know what to aim her camera at next.

CHAPTER 20

"Video off," Batgirl ordered Harley.

"This could be important information—think of the viewers!" Harley protested. Batgirl didn't flinch. She wasn't as fun without the hat, Harley noted as she shut off her camera.

"Miss Martian, tell everyone what you know," Batgirl said.

Miss Martian willed herself to be seen, and several Supers gathered around her. "The hats are controlling—or at least influencing—everyone. But not in the same way. Some people are happy, others are belligerent, and still others are just flat-out wacky. It's as if someone wants everyone to act crazy."

"Well, it is the KRAZY Karnival," Harley joked.

No one laughed.

"So, what's our plan?" asked Miss Martian. "We have a plan, right?"

"We confiscate all remaining hats," said Batgirl. "Supers first."

"But we have to break the bubble that's trapping us in here," Wonder Woman noted. "Lois Lane is reporting that the Green Team is robbing every house and business in Metropolis."

"Yes, but with all of us Supers working together, it will be easier to break it," Poison Ivy said.

"Someone plotted to have us trapped in here," Hawkgirl chimed in. "But who?"

"The Junior Detective Society will figure out who and why," said Batgirl.

"But first, this," Harley interrupted. She turned the camera on. "This is the REAL Harley Quinn here, assuring you that the super heroes of Super Hero High will be in Metropolis soon to help save the day from the Green Team, who's—"

The screen sizzled with static. Fake Harley suddenly appeared. "To save the day, we have the Green Team, a group of talented teens. And back in the bubble, let's watch the Krazy Karnival! I guarantee, you've never seen anything like it before!"

"Why did you just say that?" Beast Boy asked Harley. "That was totally not the right thing to say!"

"It wasn't me!" Harley yelled, leaning in toward Beast Boy's face. "I wouldn't do that!"

"You just did!" he yelled back.

"We can discuss this later," said Wonder Woman, breaking the two up. "Right now we have work to do. Let's go get all those hats!"

"Some of us should stay back and try to figure out who's behind this," Bumblebee said.

"Great idea," said Hawkgirl. "Miss Martian, we'll need you here with us. Harley, stay in contact. I'd say that someone's out to get you. The fake Harley is proof of that."

"Proof, schmoof." Harley gripped her mallet. "Let them try," she said. "I'll show 'em why it's not smart to mess with Harley Quinn!"

As the hat-free Supers zeroed in on their classmates still wearing hats, Beast Boy spotted Cheetah.

"Hey there, Cheetah, you sure look nice today," he said.

Cheetah absentmindedly touched her beret. "Why, thank you, Beast Boy, and so do . . ."

But before she could finish her sentence, Beast Boy had transformed into an eagle, snatched Cheetah's hat with his beak, and was flying circles above her.

"You—you stole my hat, you green pest," Cheetah said accusingly.

"You're welcome," Beast Boy replied as he handed the hat

off mid-flight to Adam Strange, who then tossed it to Starfire, who dropped it toward Katana, who sliced it in half before it touched the ground.

"Cheetah," Harley said, lowering her voice. "You were being nice . . . to everyone."

Cheetah looked startled, and then she scowled like she had just sucked on a lemon.

With each hat confiscated and destroyed, the Supers gained momentum and Batgirl crossed another name off the list. Working together, they found gathering the hats from the Krazy Karnival guests was easy . . . almost. Captain Cold was particularly hard to separate from his pirate hat. But once hatless, he was back to his ornery self.

"Someone was trying to control my mind?" he said, seething. "That's not cool!"

"The hat was controlling my mind?" Lady Shiva repeated as she stared at the smoldering pile of felt and electronics at her feet. El Diablo and Sapphire had confiscated her hat; then El Diablo had hit it with flames. One by one, as each Super's head cleared, they began to understand what had happened.

Meanwhile, when it finally dawned on guests that they had been under some sort of mind control, panic began to spread. Confusion built to epic proportions, especially when they tried to escape from the Krazy Karnival and learned that there was no way out of the bubble.

"Nothing good can come of this," Fake Harley reported. "I love it!"

"That's not me!" Real Harley said, interrupting Fake Harley's feed. Suddenly the video cut to one of the remote cameras that Harley had put up earlier.

On the screen, Wonder Woman was swooping toward the Tunnel of Love, where she was met in the sky by Silver Swan. Each hovered in the air, neither speaking. Silver Swan did a pirouette so fast she had to hold on to her hat, to keep it from flying off. When she stopped, she glared at Wonder Woman, who returned her unblinking stare.

"Please give me your hat," Wonder Woman said evenly.

On the ground below them, The Flash, the last Super Hero High student with a hat still on his head, was being chased by several Supers.

"Why would I want to do that?" Silver Swan scoffed.

"Because it's controlling your mind," Wonder Woman explained.

"No one controls Silver Swan," she said. "If you want my hat, you're going to have to take it from me."

"Oh, you don't want that," Wonder Woman warned.

"Try me," Silver Swan dared her.

Wonder Woman flung her lasso at Silver Swan. But before it reached her, Silver Swan began to hum, slowing the lasso's projection. Then she let out a powerful sound wave that made the lasso snap back toward Wonder Woman.

"Oops!" said Silver Swan. "Maybe you aren't as invincible as they say you are."

Wonder Woman brushed off the comment and tightened her grip on the Lasso of Truth. "I guess we're going to have to find out," she said, flying full force at her nemesis.

Silver Swan pirouetted once more then retreated into the Tunnel of Love with Wonder Woman in pursuit.

"We can't see what's going on inside," Harley said over the video as the scene projected onto the screens all across the carnival. "But something's sure happening!"

Only the sounds of battle could be heard. Smashes and crashes abounded. At times, swan boats flew out of the entrance and exit, barely missing bystanders. Every now and then, Silver Swan flew out of the tunnel, followed closely by Wonder Woman . . . or Wonder Woman flew out with Silver Swan in pursuit, and then they both disappeared back into the tunnel. Things were happening so fast, no one could keep up with either combatant.

Suddenly, there was quiet.

No one moved. All over the amusement park and beyond, viewers were riveted to the screens.

Where was Silver Swan? And more importantly, where was Wonder Woman?

CHAPTER 21

They couldn't see anything, but they could hear a beautiful low hum coming from the tunnel. It was Silver Swan. Harley stared at the video monitor. There was a murmur from the crowd outside of what was left of the Tunnel of Love. Where was Wonder Woman?

A rustle of wings signaled Silver Swan, who emerged smiling. Hawkgirl and Poison Ivy gasped.

It was Batgirl who began cheering first. "There she is, right behind Silver Swan," she said, pointing at the screen. "Wonder Woman's got the Lasso of Truth around Silver Swan!"

"Look what's in her other hand!" shouted Hawkgirl.

Sure enough, Wonder Woman was holding a hat.

"I wasn't keen on wearing it," Silver Swan was saying as she rubbed her forehead. "But he insisted. He said everyone at the carnival had to wear the hats."

The video was suddenly fuzzy as Fake Harley took control.

"You saw it here first," she said, winking. "Silver Swan was unemployed until J.J. Tetch, the kind owner of Krazy Karnival, gave her a job. But the real story is that those teens from Super Hero High will soon be out of work. They're stealing hats, of all things!" Fake Harley looked straight into the camera and confided, "I never did like any of my schoolmates. They're a sneaky bunch!"

"Harley!" said Poison Ivy, looking aghast. "How can you say that?"

"It's not me!" Harley reminded her. "It's the FAKE me."

"Oops, sorry," Poison Ivy said sheepishly.

"So it's J.J. Tetch behind all this," The Flash noted, still befuddled from the chase and having his hat removed.

"I think we all suspected that," Batgirl said.

"But the real question is why," Hawkgirl added.

"And what does he have against me?" lamented Harley. "He was so nice!"

"I'm sure it has something to do with the Green Team," Batgirl deduced. "Lois is saying that their looting is getting worse, and their team is multiplying."

"Why would anyone want to do math at a time like this?" Harley quipped. Most of the heroes rolled their eyes while she snickered at her own joke.

"Harley, plug me in to the cameras you have all over the carnival. I want to see what's going on," Batgirl said.

Harley and Batgirl sat side by side, Batgirl with her

computer, Harley with her video control panel. The others looked over their shoulders.

"I think all hats are accounted for, except for the ones from the carnival workers," Supergirl said to Big Barda. "The civilians are still calming down, and the super heroes from the other schools are all on board with helping us. Together we'll get the hats from the workers. So far they've refused to give them up of their own accord. It appears that J.J. hired a bunch of thugs and villains."

Harley hit the "On" button on her camera and was about to broadcast, but someone beat her to it. "Oh, my! What if there's a surprise in store for those super heroes? Like maybe a battle in the bubble!" Fake Harley said gleefully. "Whatever's up next is sure to be epic! Tell everyone to tune in."

"Hey!" Real Harley cried. "That's what I was going to say!"

Hawkgirl said, "You know things are totally crazy when Fake Harley and Real Harley are saying the same thing."

"Let's give it another try," suggested Wonder Woman as the Supers rallied. "We've moved mountains, we've fought epic battles, we've conquered evil. Breaking a bubble shouldn't be all that hard."

Others followed her lead as she hurled her shield against the bubble. Bumblebee used her blasters, Supergirl used her heat vision, and Big Barda threw her mega-rod with all her might. But the bubble didn't even budge.

"Okay," Harley said. She was hopping up and down with an excess of energy. "Plan B. We fan out and track down J.J. Once we get him, we find out what his motives are and how to get out of here. Everyone, pair up!"

The carousel riders were relieved when Batgirl fixed the mechanics and slowed it down. Harley and Batgirl then bypassed the Rock 'n' Roller Coaster when they saw that Hawkgirl and Ivy had it under control.

"How's about going in there?" Harley said, pointing to the House of Mirrors. She didn't wait for Batgirl's answer. It was as if it was calling to her. *Harley . . .*

It was cool in the darkness. Before Batgirl could activate her flashlight, the room was flooded with light so bright that both girls had to shield their eyes.

Harley peeked through her fingers. "Whoa!"

Batgirl squinted. "Ditto!" she said as she took in the hundreds of reflections. "Are you seeing what I'm seeing?"

"A whole lot of Harleys?" Harley said.

"Yes, but only one of me," Batgirl noted. "The mirrors are

only showing *your* reflection."

Harley looked around. Sure enough, there were Harleys everywhere, but no Batgirls, other than the one standing next to her.

Harley turned on her shoulder cam. "I think I'm gonna want footage of this," she said as the red light blinked.

"It's like a Harley Quinn convention!" Batgirl exclaimed.

"I'd go to that," Harley said. She stopped again to look at herself in the mirror. "Uh, Batgirl?"

"Yes?" said Batgirl, who was taking a moment for reports from Metropolis. The city was now on lockdown.

"I think I just winked at myself," Harley said.

"Oh . . . kay?" Batgirl said then returned her attention to their immediate situation. "Let's keep an eye out for strange happenings."

"The wink was a strange happening," said Harley. "Because my image winked at me, but I didn't do any winking." She started making faces and then began a series of somersaults and flips, watching herself in the mirror.

"What are you doing?" Batgirl asked, perplexed. "This is not the time to create new gymnastics routines."

Harley did a complicated triple flip, but at the last second, reversed it, and yelled, "Can you do that?"

The Harley in the mirror just smiled and stood still.

At the same time, Batgirl and Harley shouted, "FAKE HARLEY!"

Harley began smashing the mirrors with her mallet. As each mirror shattered, the Harley reflected there disappeared.

"One of the mirrors isn't really a mirror. That fake is in the room with us," Harley cried. "I'm going to find this pretender. There's only one Harley Quinn!"

"That's for sure," Batgirl said as she removed a Batarang from her utility belt and tossed it, causing mirrors to fall onto each other and break.

There was glass everywhere, but it seemed that for every mirror that broke, there was another to take its place. During it all, Fake Harley began taunting them, saying, "Catch me if you can!"

"Fake!" Harley cried in frustration. She swung her mallet hard and shattered another mirror into hundreds of tiny shards of glass. Then she froze. "Um, Batgirl?" she called. "Can you come here, please? I think you're gonna want to see this."

CHAPTER 22

"Your hat, miss," the man said, smiling. He held out a jester's hat of many colors with a golden bell on the top. "A gift from J.J."

Harley's eyes locked on the equalizer in the man's other hand. It had mirrors on the end of it, and reminded of her of the trifold mirrors in a department-store dressing room.

"No, thank you," Harley said. "I don't wanna muss up my hair." She poufed up one of her pigtails.

"I see you brought a friend to the party," he said, bowing slightly. "How do you do? I'm Mirror Master." Though he had on a green hood and cowl, a white sailor hat with a first-mate insignia sat snug on his head, looking out of place.

"I know who you are," Batgirl answered. "You use ultra-advanced mirror technology to create holograms, like the one you made of Fake Harley. But what I don't understand is how you were able to make it so convincing."

"Yeah, confess—or say hello to this," Harley said, raising her mallet in the air.

"Well, you liked the mirror I sent you, right?" he asked. He was taller than both girls by almost two feet, and muscular.

"What mirror?" Harley asked. Her eyes flickered with recognition. She touched her pocket. "Oh, that mirror!"

"Yes, the hand mirror was from me," he said, smugly. "Thought you'd like it. Who doesn't like to look at themselves? I know I do." He glanced at a mirror and admired himself.

"I get it now," Batgirl said, nodding. "Harley, every time you looked in the mirror he was image-mapping you. Your looks, your movement, your quirks. Plus, he was collecting everything you've ever said so Fake Harley could have a speech bank to draw from."

Harley gulped. "Ya mean ya heard what I was saying when I was alone?"

Mirror Master smiled. "That I did, Harley! That I did."

"How unoriginal," Batgirl said. "You're just a copycat."

"Oh, dear. Are you trying to hurt my feelings?" Mirror Master said, feigning sadness. "I'm more than a copycat. And to prove it, maybe I'll create an army of Batgirls next."

Harley gasped. "The Green Team! That's why there are so many of them. You did that!"

"She's catching on," Mirror Master said. "Good for you, Harley." He tapped his equalizer. "I can control reflections and mirror images from here.

"What is it that you want?" Harley asked.

"I want a good job review," Mirror Master said. "I want to make the boss happy. Fake Harley was my idea," he boasted. "He loved that!"

"Please tell us more," Batgirl said, flattering him.

"Well, remember when you two created those HarleyGrams?" Both nodded. Batgirl had helped Harley make small holographic images of herself to help promote Harley's Quinntessentials. "I thought, I can do better than that! So I created a walking, talking reflection of Harley. One that can be programmed by me. At the same time, I can use my mirror skills to make it look like the Green Team is multiplying and cause confusion and panic everywhere."

"He's a genius," Fake Harley said.

"Harley, meet Harley," Mirror Master said smugly. "Now, who's ready for some fun?"

Harley raised her mallet in the air at the same time Fake Harley did. As Mirror Master laughed, he didn't see Batgirl slip away. Real Harley and Fake Harley were swinging their mallets so fast and doing such astonishing gymnastics moves that it was impossible to tell which one was real.

"Get her!" Mirror Master ordered Fake Harley. "Use Harley's own techniques of speed, strength, and gymnastics on her. My Harley can do everything you can do," he boasted to the real Harley. "Only, here, my Harley has the advantage."

It was true. With her reflection everywhere, Harley couldn't tell just who she was fighting. She was swinging madly, hitting every image of herself.

"Not even you can tell the difference between yourself and a fake," Mirror Master bragged.

Harley paused. "You are so right. Thank you for the tip!"

As she ran around the room doing backflips and cartwheels, Fake Harley did the same. They moved so fast they blurred together. When they stopped, both faced Mirror Master.

"Stop playing around," he ordered. "Get her!"

"Get her!" both Harleys yelled. "Get Harley!"

Harley starting mimicking the fake version of herself. If she couldn't tell the difference, there was no way Mirror Master could either.

Step by step, backflip by backflip, triple sidewinder by triple sidewinder, the Harleys did the same thing. They were mirror images of each other—and their reflections filled the House of Mirrors.

"I see what you're doing," he said. "You can't fool me."

What he didn't see was that Batgirl had returned, and she had someone with her.

CHAPTER 23

Harley spied Batgirl and The Flash sneaking behind the mirrors. She wanted to call out to them, but if she did, Mirror Master would also know where she was.

Batgirl kept staring down at something small in her hand: her B.A.T. heat-seeking device. There was only one Harley in the room who had a temperature and a heartbeat.

Mirror Master punched some buttons on the side of his equalizer. Instantly, Fake Harley started saying, "It's me, Harley Quinn, and you're watching the all-Harley all-the-time Harley's Quinntessentials! I'm the real deal!"

As the fake kept repeating this, so did the real Harley. She knew that confusion was often key in apprehending a villain. She had learned this in Commissioner Gordon's Understanding the Criminal Mind class.

The mirrors in the room and all the shattered pieces reflected Fake Harley and Real Harley. It was beyond confusing. "Let's dance!" Harley said to her doppelgänger.

The two began to spin around, reflecting each other's moves perfectly.

If the Harleys had competed in the dance contest, surely they would have won. Both gripped their mallets and held them out to their sides. With each spin, more mirrors shattered, leaving a trail of broken glass.

Mirror Master had been so focused on the Harleys that he didn't see Batgirl and The Flash sneak up on him. Suddenly, a streak of red rushed by.

"I got it!" yelled The Flash, holding up Mirror Master's mirror equalizer and tossing it upward.

"No, *I* got it!" growled Mirror Master as he lunged for it.

"No, *I* got it!" said Batgirl triumphantly from the ceiling, where she was perched upside down. She dangled the equalizer from her B.A.T. wire.

"Give that to me!" Mirror Master demanded.

"Okay, but first let me take a look," Batgirl said.

"Hellooooooo!" Harley called out. She was still spinning around the room with Fake Harley. "I love to dance, but this is makin' me dizzy!"

Batgirl quickly reprogrammed the Mirror Master's equalizer, and suddenly, Fake Harley stopped dancing. "Phew!" Harley said as they both wobbled. "I was runnin' out of dance moves."

"Harley, say goodbye to Harley," Batgirl said as she punched more buttons on the equalizer.

"Bye-bye," Harley said as Fake Harley disappeared with a digital *ping*. "And don't come back!"

"What have you done?" Mirror Master yelled. "I'm going to get in so much trouble now!"

By then The Flash had tied him up with a length of blinking carnival lights. Batgirl removed the sailor hat from Mirror Master's head. "Who are you working for?" she demanded.

"I don't work for anyone," he said. "Hey, does anyone have an aspirin? I have a huge headache."

"It's J.J., isn't it?" asked Batgirl.

"I don't feel good," Mirror Master moaned. "Stop asking me questions!"

The Flash held on to the lights that bound the Mirror Master as they led him to the Lost and Found area, where the other carnival workers were being held. "Got another one!" he called out.

Miss Martian was standing off to the side, her eyes closed. "They're all thinking the same thing," she said.

"What's that?" Harley asked.

"Mad Hatter," Miss Martian said. "That's the name that keeps coming up when the carnival workers' hats come off."

"**WOWZA!**" Harley declared. "J.J. and Mad Hatter are the same person. That sneak!" She tapped the side of her head. "Everyone, quiet! I'm getting an idea, and it's a doozy! We get Mad Hatter, we get out of this bubble. We get out of this bubble, we save Metropolis. We save Metropolis, and I get exclusive footage! This Fake Harley business is old news. Although, it was cool having a sister, if only for a while."

"You can borrow mine," Thunder and Lightning said at the same time, then both burst out laughing.

"Well, there's only one real Harley Quinn," Harley said, dropping the mirror on the ground and raising her mallet. "I won't be needing this anymore!"

Harley was about to smash it when Batgirl stopped her. "Mind if I take that?" she asked.

Miss Martian scurried to keep up with Batgirl and Harley. "I should have guessed J.J. and Mad Hatter were one and the same. Mad Hatter can get people to do his bidding by using mind control," she explained. "The secret is his hat. The high-tech gizmos and gadgets in it enhance his powers."

"But Mirror Master is so strong, you'd think he could fight off this pest's mind games," Harley said.

Batgirl nodded. "Mirror Master may be physically strong and have the mirror tech, but he's no match for Mad Hatter's brains. And when someone wears one of his hats, Hatter's got even more control over them. It would take a person with incredible mental discipline to withstand his mind games. Look what happened to all the Supers!"

"He's close," Miss Martian said, slowing down. "I wish I could home in on him, but his thoughts are jumbled and I can't get a clean read. Wait . . . I'm getting stronger and stronger vibes. There!" She pointed to the Amazing Maze.

The sign outside the Amazing Maze was lit up. Strobe lights made it look like a neon fireworks display. But with each step closer, a bank of lights would burn out with a sizzle and fizzle into darkness. By the time they were at the entrance, the marquee was practically dark.

"Let's storm the place!" Harley suggested.

"Oh, um. Do we have to?" Miss Martian squeezed her eyes shut. Then she said to herself, "Yes, we do, Miss Martian. Get ahold of yourself." Her eyes fluttered open. "Get ahold of yourself!" she repeated, louder.

"What's going on?" asked Harley.

"I'm getting a strong signal, and if I concentrate really hard, I can get a sense of Mad Hatter's thoughts!"

"What's he thinking?" Batgirl asked.

Miss Martian closed her eyes again. "His mind is difficult to read, but it is clear he wants to see Harley, alone. Just the two of them."

"That's weird," Harley said. "I was thinking the exact same thing!"

CHAPTER 24

It had taken some convincing to get Batgirl and Miss Martian to stay behind, but in the end Harley won. "Mad Hatter just wants me," she reasoned. "If the three of us appear, he may not show up."

Silently, Harley tiptoed into the Amazing Maze. It was dark and eerily quiet, and reminded her of when she was little and used to play hide-and-seek. She would hide in the closet, sometimes falling asleep when no one found her.

Though Harley was usually boisterous and brave, she could feel her heart beat faster and faster. As she got closer to danger, it excited and scared her at the same time. Suddenly a projectile flew at her. Harley whipped her mallet around like a baseball bat, smashing it.

"Oh dear, why did you do that?" A friendly voice from above asked as pieces of candied apple rained down. "Is that any way to treat a gift?"

Before Harley could say anything, something caught her

attention. Across the room, at end of a long hallway, was a sign beckoning her.

ON AIR, the red neon flashed. *ON AIR.*

Harley made her way down the corridor, which got narrower and narrower with each step. Finally, it spilled into a cavernous room.

The maze walls rose twelve feet high, too tall for Harley to see over. Taking a deep breath, she sprinted head-on toward one, using momentum to run up the side, flip herself over, and grab the ledge with two hands. Doing a pull-up, Harley peered over the top. She saw nothing but maze and more maze.

Undaunted, she let go and continued her journey, wandering through the winding labyrinth, doubling back whenever she hit a dead end.

"What's taking you so long?" Mad Hatter asked impatiently, his voice booming over a loudspeaker.

"I'm in no hurry, J.J.," Harley replied, careful to sound confident, even if she didn't feel that way. The maze was so confusing. Had she already walked this way? Everything looked the same. "Or do you go by Mad Hatter?"

"Oh, you can call me Mad Hatter," he said, letting out a long, gleeful laugh. "Although some people just call me mad!"

"I'd like to call you . . . when you're in prison," Harley quipped.

"What's that? I can't hear you," Mad Hatter said. "What's the matter, Harley? I thought you'd be better at hide-and-seek."

Harley looked around. The maze walls were a glaring white. She wished she had sunglasses. That's when she looked up.

"You're pretty quiet," Mad Hatter said. "That's not like you. What's the matter? Scared?"

"Scared, schmared. I'm not afraid of the likes of you," she said, shaking the inkling of self-doubt that had crept into her brain. Harley was used to having other Supers around her, backing each other up. But this was to be a solo performance. "Focus, Harley," she reminded herself. She thought, *What would Batgirl do?*

Harley fumbled around in her pocket. It was still there—the little box from her friend. She opened it and smiled. Inside was the teeny-tiny QuinnCam drone camera. Harley slipped on the ring that controlled it—and the drone. She wished Batgirl had also given her instructions. Then she noticed that when she moved her ring finger, the QuinnCam moved too. When Harley pointed the ring to the left, the camera turned left. When she pointed it to the right, it went right. And if she moved her hand up and pointed the ring skyward, that was where the camera went.

Harley looked at the ring and could see what the camera was recording on a small screen built into the ring. She had a view of the entire maze! But where was Mad Hatter? Harley rotated the ring until—at last—she found what she was looking for.

She made the little drone rise a little bit higher, out of sight. She had a feeling it might come in handy later.

He was sitting on what looked like a red velvet throne in the middle of the maze, sipping from a dainty blue teacup. Harley nimbly wove her way around, using the images from the drone camera overhead as her guide. Finally, there was only a wall between them.

"Where are you, Harley Quinn?" Mad Hatter's voice was almost a singsong. "You're not scared, are you? I'd think someone of your stature, of your skills, and of your presence, wouldn't be scared of anything. Reveal yourself! I have a proposition to make!"

Harley took a step back, did a couple of sidewinders, and then ran up, up . . . and over the wall, landing in front of Mad Hatter. "Ta-da! Here I am! Didja miss me?" she said, looking fierce. "Now, what's so all-fired important, before I take you in?"

Mad Hatter didn't look surprised. In fact, he looked amused, as if he had anticipated this moment.

"Harley!" he said, clasping his hands with joy. "So glad

that we can have this moment together."

Though the maze walls had been austere white, where Mad Hatter sat looked like a cozy living room, complete with a fireplace. Harley's stomach made a loud growling sound, reminding her she hadn't eaten lunch.

Laid out before her was a feast of colorful carnival food. Harley's eyes stopped at the sugar-and-cinnamon-powdered funnel cakes stacked so high they threatened to topple.

As if reading her mind, Mad Hatter said, "This is all for you. Sit, sit, Harley. Have some cake and tea, have whatever you'd like. We have so much to talk about, you and me. We are much more alike than you realize."

CHAPTER 25

Harley stood warily. Mad Hatter didn't seem to have any bodyguards or villains at his side, and there were no weapons that she could see. *What does he want?* she wondered. Perhaps it really was Mirror Master who was the villain, and he had been using Mad Hatter this whole time. After all, the man sitting in front of her seemed harmless.

The funnel cakes looked delicious, and Harley was hungry. "Maybe just one bite," she said, picking up a gold plate. The initials *MH* were written in the center in cursive.

Mad Hatter rubbed his hands together and encouraged Harley to pile her plate high with treats. "More! More! Take more!" he said. "More is better!"

"Thisissogood!" Harley gushed after taking a bite. Crisp on the outside, the funnel cake was soft and warm inside. Harley made a mental note to tell Bumblebee about it. Surely it would taste even better drizzled with honey.

"Please sit, Harley," her genial host insisted.

As Harley joined him, she set her mallet aside, making sure she could grab it if needed. Harley tried to remember what Commissioner Gordon had told his students about getting information from a criminal.

Harley watched Mad Hatter adjust his oversized top hat. It was green with a band of yellow around the base, and boasted a wide brim that didn't detract from the fancy deep blue stitching. It tipped to one side, making Mad Hatter look slightly lopsided, and the sparkles and lights were mesmerizing. Harley recalled that Miss Martian had said something about his hat. But what?

Well, it'll come to me, Harley thought. She'd never had a shortage of ideas.

Mad Hatter poured her a glass of iced tea. She drained it in one long swallow. She hadn't realized how thirsty she was. Harley wiped her mouth with the back of her hand, trying to remember why she was there. Perhaps it was to Save the Day, or the world. Or maybe to unmuddle the mystery of the big bubble and unmask the true villain. Was it Mirror Master or Mad Hatter ... or someone else completely? Harley was confused. She wished she was as sleuthy as the Junior Detectives. Then again, there were some things she was terribly good at, like running Harley's Quinntessentials!

"Hey, Mr. Hatter," Harley said, trying to focus. Her thoughts were whirling around. She got up and poked at his hat with her index finger. "That's some amazing *chapeau* you got there. *Chapeau*—that's French for 'hat'!"

The smile slid off his face for a moment before he laughed and said, "Oh, Harley, you crack me up. *Merci!* Thank you for the French lesson."

Both of his hands gripped the edge of his hat as he secured it tightly on his head. Luckily, Harley wasn't wearing a hat. There was nothing he could do to her, she thought.

"Do you know who your biggest fan is?" Mad Hatter asked playfully. "Care to guess?"

"One of my viewers? Wait. I know . . . that lady who sends me pictures of her grandkids?"

Mad Hatter laughed good-naturedly. "No, not them. Though you do have legions of admirers. But your biggest fan? You're looking at him! I did this all for you, Harley Quinn! The Karnival, the Green Team—it was all to get you here and for us to talk."

"The Big Bubble?" Harley asked.

"Yes, the Big Bubble!" Mad Hatter said, puffing himself up. "Oh, Ms. Quinn, you've figured it out!"

"I have?" Harley was used to people saying she was funny, and that she could do the best acrobatics. But no one had ever pegged Harley Quinn as an intellectual. "You think I'm smart?" she asked, flattered.

"Of course you are," Mad Hatter said. "You are are remarkably smart."

Harley's brain was on overdrive. "Okay, so as I see it, you

worked with Mirror Master to duplicate the Green Team and make their mirror images rob Metropolis."

He looked at her admiringly. "See?" Mad Hatter leaned over and tapped Harley's forehead. "Smart thinking. But I didn't do this just to rob Metropolis. That's child's play. Any common criminal can do that."

"I—I don't understand," Harley sputtered. She was so confused, she stopped eating cake.

"Please, get comfortable and I'll tell you why," Mad Hatter said. "I have been a fan of yours ever since you started Harley's Quinntessentials. In fact, I was one of your very first viewers. MH234. Recognize that?"

"MH234? That's you?" Harley exclaimed, her eyes wide. "MH234 is always the first to cheer me up when things go wrong!"

Mad Hatter beamed, wickedly delighted. "That's me. Remember the time you crashed the Internet?" Harley nodded. How could she forget that? Everyone was mad at her. Well ... almost everyone. "Do you remember what MH234 said?" he asked, wagging a finger at her.

"MH234 said, 'You're just getting started, Harley Quinn. Keep going. Someday you're going to be big!'" she quoted. She had memorized lots of MH234's messages.

Mad Hatter burst out laughing. Harley liked the way his eyes sparkled. "Was I right, or was I right?" he asked.

"You, sir, were right!" Harley said, biting into a treat.

"I believe in you, Harley," Mad Hatter said sincerely. "And even more now that we've met. You know, we should work together."

"How?" she asked.

Mad Hatter stared into her eyes. "I love your Web shows. You're so innovative. I mean, c'mon. That dance contest? The Super Bloopers, where the super heroes mess up? The 'Ask Harley' segment? Brilliant. All of them!"

Harley liked what she was hearing.

"May I ask ya something, Mr. Hatter?"

"Anything, anything for you, my dear," he answered.

"How would we work together? I'm not saying that we would, but if we did, how would that be?" she asked.

Mad Hatter set his teacup down. "When we team up you will be the top media superstar in the world! With your personality and viewership, and my skills at marketing and planning—"

"Go on," Harley urged. This was getting interesting.

"Where is Mirror Master?" Mad Hatter suddenly asked, looking around. "He has a present for you! MIRROR MASTER!"

Harley tried not to smile. She knew Mad Hatter was in for a surprise when he found out that Mirror Master was in custody.

It was Harley Quinn who was surprised.

Mirror Master was standing in front of her. When she last saw him, he was in custody and being hauled away by The Flash toward the Lost and Found, where the Supers were guarding the criminals.

"Where have you been?" Mad Hatter asked. Harley thought she saw his eyes flicker with disapproval. When she looked again, he was greeting Mirror Master with a toothy smile. "Do you have the present for Ms. Quinn, here? That special one."

"I do!" Mirror Master said. He held his mirror equalizer in one hand . . . and a hat in the other.

Harley recognized it as the one he'd tried to give her earlier: the eccentric jester-hat-of-many-colors, adorned with jingly-jangly bells.

"For you, my dear Ms. Quinn," Mad Hatter said, bowing to her. He took the hat from Mirror Master and held it high above Harley's head, as if about to crown her.

She looked nervously at Mirror Master. His jaw was tight. He kept his mirror equalizer aimed right at her. Harley's mallet lay on the ground. She reached for it, but Mirror Master kicked it out of reach and held up his equalizer.

Mad Hatter had a delighted look on his face. "Oh, pshaw! We won't need that," he said to Mirror Master. "Put that thing away. Harley's on our team now, or at least she will be soon!"

Harley gripped the side of the chair as Mad Hatter slowly lowered the hat on her head, making sure it was on tight. "Now, that's better," he said, grinning. "You look great!"

Harley's eyes glazed over. She opened her mouth to speak but nothing came out. Finally she said, "It. Fits. Great. We are a great fit, too."

"Oh, Harley!" Mad Hatter crowed. "Think of the two of us together. What a team we'd make! Hatter and Harley!"

"Harley and Hatter," she began to correct him.

He chuckled good-naturedly. "You are right. You're the star! It should be Harley and Hatter! One has to be flexible about these things, you know."

Harley cocked her head. She was getting signals from the hat. Warm, fuzzy signals. They were telling her things. "Okay!" she shouted, then calmed down. "Okay, Mr. Hatter. Working with you will be like a dream."

Mad Hatter whispered to Mirror Master, "My mind-control hats work every time! But hats can only go so far. And it's so much work to get people to wear them. However, with this girl, well . . ."

He turned to Harley. "I'm your biggest fan. Harley's Quinntessentials has the built-in audience to get me started on the road to fame and fortune—my fame and my fortune.

Now I can mind-control the masses when they tune in. Everyone will be watching you, and that means they'll be seeing me, too. Everyone. Everywhere! And when they do, I'll rob them blind, and they will love me for it!"

Harley nodded slowly. "Mind-control the masses!" she repeated robotically. "How?"

Mad Hatter poured himself more tea. He dropped several lumps of sugar into it and stirred slowly. "Simple," he explained. "This is the new wave of crime. No more robbing banks and stores. That's so old-school—plus, it can get messy. With Hatter and Harley, we will just tell everyone to send us their money and gems and jewels, and whatever we want! And they will because they will have no choice once they're tuned in to us. I'm going to mesmerize them via mass media!"

Harley's head was buzzing.

"I am so glad you came to your senses, my dear," Mad Hatter was saying. "Even if I did have to give you a little nudge with that hat. And by the way, it looks marvelous on you. Your fans will love it. You and I are so much alike. We both want to be adored by the masses and will do anything to get what we crave: all eyes on us!"

He smiled warmly and settled back in his chair to take a congratulatory sip of tea. Mad Hatter reveled in the moment, then leaned forward and asked, "What do you say, Ms. Quinn? Shall we shake hands to seal our partnership?"

Harley stood up. She held out her hand. Mirror Master looked on from the sidelines, still aiming his equalizer at her.

"Okey-dokey, Mr. Hatter," Harley said, extending her hand. "Let's do this!"

Harley and Mad Hatter gripped hands and shook, but she wouldn't let go, gripping tighter and tighter. Then Harley began to laugh. Softly at first, then louder and louder.

CHAPTER 26

"*What?!*" Mad Hatter roared. "Mirror Master! Get Harley!"

Mirror Master raised his mirror equalizer.

"Go ahead, zap me," Harley dared him as she tightened her grip on Mad Hatter.

Mad Hatter looked from Mirror Master to Harley, then back again. His eyes narrowed and his jaw tightened. "Zap her!" Mad Hatter demanded. "Do it now!"

"Yes, boss," Mirror Master said, taking aim.

Harley didn't even flinch when Mirror Master squeezed the trigger.

BOOM!

When the puff of vanilla-scented smoke cleared, colorful confetti and streamers rained down on them.

Mad Hatter was stunned.

Harley could not stop laughing.

"Oh, that's not the real Mirror Master," she said."I knew when Mirror Master showed up that it couldn't be the real thing. Batgirl and The Flash would never let him escape—so this guy had to be a fake!"

"The jester hat . . . ," Mad Hatter started to say.

"Ooh, you're so smart, Mr. H!" Harley said, tapping his forehead. "Yep. That's why I put on the hat. I also knew my friends wouldn't allow me to fall under your mind control."

"What?" Mad Hatter sputtered.

"Oopsie, sorry," Harley said, not sounding sorry in the least. "I forgot to tell you something important. Something really, awfully, terribly, superly important!"

"What?" he growled.

Harley paused, then smiled. "I've been broadcasting our little talk—to the whole world!" She waved to the QuinnCam hovering above.

Mad Hatter finally noticed the small drone sparkling in the dark. He was speechless.

"Aren't you gonna say anything? Congrats! You're suddenly famous—but your fifteen minutes are up, in about"—she checked her watch—"in about six minutes. And now it's my responsibility to see that you're put away where you belong . . . in prison!"

Mad Hatter's coloring went from red to white to green, and then back to its regular pale self. He cleared his throat and lowered his voice. "Listen to me, Harley. We're a team, remember? Hatter and Harley, er . . . Harley and Hatter. Just put me in front of the camera and tell everyone to stare at their screens. We will have the biggest audience in the history of the world. You will be the most famous person on the planet! Everyone's going to want to know what the two of us now have in store for them.

"Harley," he whispered. "We can say that the little scene they just witnessed was a prank. A joke!" He forced a laugh. "Like when you did 'Where's Harley?' Then we can rule the airwaves . . . and the world!"

Harley thought about this. She had always wanted more, more, more. More viewers, more fame, more everything. And now was her chance. Mad Hatter was handing it to her.

Harley looked directly up at the QuinnCam, took a deep breath, and said, "Hey, Harley's Quinntessentials viewers. This is really hard for me to say. But I've made my decision. Thank you for watching, but a girl's gotta do what a girl's gotta do."

Mad Hatter grinned and winked at Harley. He puffed himself up, but his smile quickly turned into a look of terror. "Nooo!" he cried as Harley grabbed her mallet. With one smooth swing, she threw it at the QuinnCam camera, smashing it to pieces.

All over the Krazy Karnival and beyond, Harley's Quinntessentials went dark.

CHAPTER 27

"Now it's just between you and me," Harley said, staring down Mad Hatter. "Let's leave the rest of the world out of this. You think I'd even consider teaming up with the likes of you? Uh, excuse me, but no!"

Mad Hatter stood up and wagged his finger in her face. "You want a fight, I'll give you one!" he shouted.

"Catch me if you can!" Harley said gleefully. Then she lowered her voice. "Guide me outta here, Batgirl!"

"Gladly, Harley," Batgirl said via the two-way communication device she had embedded in the hat. "Oh, and Miss Martian says to tell you that she's finally got a lock on reading Mad Hatter's mind, but her reception is fuzzy. She says don't ever trust him. Mad Hatter seriously thought you'd be a great team and now he's out for revenge."

"Am I going too fast for you, Mr. Hatter?" Harley said, laughing as she grabbed her mallet and weaved her way out of the maze. "Ya know, I like to make people laugh, but just as much of the time, I seem to make people upset. And boy, you look really, totally, and impressively upset right now." Harley slowed down. "Try to keep up, why don't you?"

Mad Hatter was in pursuit, but not nearly as fast as the nimble Harley. The sun was setting outside the bubble as the two raced outside.

"**WOWZA!** Everyone is still here?" Harley asked. By now she was running up and down and loop-de-looping around the roller coaster tracks with Mad Hatter huffing and puffing behind her. She could see the carnival was as crowded as ever with people. "The bubble is still in place?"

"A confirmation on both," Batgirl said. Harley stopped to adjust her hat to hear more clearly. "We're still trying to break the bubble, but everyone is safe, and we've got the Krazy Karnival workers on lockdown while we sort out who's a true criminal and who was under mind control."

Before Harley could reply, someone grabbed her shoulder. "GOTCHA!" Mad Hatter cried triumphantly.

"No, got *you*!" she said, doing a flip and ending up standing in front of him. The tracks began to shake as a roller coaster car came barreling at them at high speed.

"Yikes!" both screamed.

Mad Hatter toppled headfirst into the roller coaster car. "See you!" he yelled to Harley, who had jumped over the car and was now standing on the tracks alone.

"Do you need backup?" Batgirl asked.

"I got this," Harley assured her. "You keep working on breaking the bubble. Mad Hatter is my battle to fight."

Mad Hatter was on the ground, holding two fistfuls of darts from the Balloon Pop game. "You won't get me if I get you first, Harley!" he yelled, tossing darts at her. But for a guy who ran a carnival, his aim was terrible, and Harley dodged the darts easily.

Harley swung off the roller coaster track, twirled in a pike position in the air, and landed on her feet in front of Mad Hatter. "I'm making this easy for you," she said. "How nice am I? Come and get me, or maybe now I should get you!"

Mad Hatter gulped as Harley swung her mallet around like she was twirling a baton, tossing it up a few times and then snatching it out of the air. She had blocked him and there was only one way he could escape. Holding on to his hat, Mad Hatter pivoted and headed toward the Ferris wheel. He grabbed on to a passenger car and was yanked off the ground.

Harley leapt and climbed up the turning wheel until she landed safely in the car Mad Hatter clung to.

"Phew! This is comfy," she said, leaning back in the seat and admiring the view.

"Help!" someone called.

She peered down to find Mad Hatter hanging to the bottom of the car with one hand.

"Harley, help me!" he pleaded. "I'm losing my grip."

"Aww, I dunno," she said. "You were pretty mean, trying to use me to control the world. That's so not cool."

"That was the old me. This is the new me," Mad Hatter insisted. He looked frightened. "Please, I'm scared."

Mad Hatter's face was drained of color. Tears puddled in his eyes. "Please, Harley," he begged as the Ferris wheel continued to go round and round and round.

She took a breath. "I'll help you so you don't fall," Harley finally said, offering him a hand, "but first you have to tell me how to break the bubble."

"Listen," Mad Hatter said as his fingers laced with hers. "Just get Obstreperous."

"Obstrep-who?" Harley asked, confused.

"Obstreperous," Mad Hatter repeated. "Harley, please," he yelled. "A deal's a deal. I just told you how to break the bubble, now save me!"

Mad Hatter's hand was shaking. Harley could feel his fear as he was about to plummet to the ground. She tightened her grip, and with an "OOMPH!" pulled him to safety. "You can thank me now," she said.

"Certainly," he replied, catching his breath. "How's about this for a thank you?"

Before Harley could say "you're welcome," Mad Hatter pushed her off the Ferris wheel.

CHAPTER 28

"Not nice!" Harley could be heard yelling as she fell from the Mad Hatter's sight. "I thought a deal was a deal!"

"Bye-bye, Harley Quinn," Mad Hatter said, flicking a piece of lint off his jacket. "Pity. We could have been great together. But no one beats Mad Hatter."

"No one but me!" said a gleeful voice. Harley pulled herself up and into the Ferris wheel car.

"How—? What—? Who—? How—?" Mad Hatter sputtered. "I pushed you. I saw you fall. . . ."

"You should have stayed tuned, Mr. Hatter." Harley pretended to look sad. "Scene one: You pushed me. Scene two: I landed in the car below. Scene three: I vaulted back up here. Why? 'Cause, duh! I'm a gymnast. It's what we do," Harley pointed out. "So, Mr. T., aka Mad Hatter, aka Mr. Soon to Be in Jail! Why don't ya tell us how to shut down your impenetrable bubble?"

Furious, Mad Hatter's face grew red as he summoned all

the powers of his hat. His eyes narrowed as he focused on Harley, who scrunched her nose at him and swatted the air between them like she was batting away a fly.

"Hey, stop that!" she ordered. "You're buggin' me!"

Harley could hear Batgirl through the jester's hat telling her to bring Mad Hatter in, but something kept interrupting her. It was Mad Hatter repeating, "You will surrender, you will surrender, you will surrender . . ."

Harley shut her eyes tight to block him out. Even though her hat had been deprogrammed and reprogrammed to sync with communications from Batgirl, Mad Hatter's hat still had some serious powers.

"Block him!" Harley could hear Batgirl yelling. "He can only mind-control someone who is vulnerable. Don't look at him. And think of something else, anything but Mad Hatter. He can't control you if you don't let him!"

Think of something else, Harley thought, scrunching her eyes closed. But what? Well, there's that. And that. Oh, and that's funny.

When the Ferris wheel car neared the ground, Mad Hatter leapt out. When Harley opened her eyes the ride was now hundreds of feet up. She took a breath and dove out. Midair, Harley placed her body into a tuck. When she neared the ground, she rolled, then jumped up, unscathed.

By then Mad Hatter had a large lead. Harley knew she had to stop him before he got to the Lost and Found where his workers were being held. Though they were without their hats, he still had powers of mind control. She may have been able to block Mad Hatter but they were already predisposed to criminal inclinations and more likely to go along with whatever he demanded of them.

In fast pursuit, Harley threw her whole body into the maddest tumble she had ever attempted. She landed on Mad Hatter's shoulders, and his hat went flying as the two of them tumbled to the ground.

As he scrambled to pick up his hat, Harley beat him to it and put her foot down right on top of it. "What's a Mad Hatter without a hat?" Harley asked, staring down at him.

Mad Hatter, who looked surprisingly small and weak without his hat, glared at her. He sighed and shrugged. "What?"

"Just mad," Harley quipped as she raised her mallet high in the air.

"No, no, no!" he shouted. "No, not that!"

With a gleam in her eyes, Harley brought her mallet crashing down with all her might. Instantly, the hat exploded with wiring, electrical components, and computer chips. It sparked colorfully for a few moments, then winked out.

Everything went dark as all the rides stopped and the lights went out.

"My hat!" Mad Hatter wailed.

"Oh, was that your hat?" Harley asked, giving him a wink.

"The one that controlled the tech here at Krazy Karnival? The one that controlled the minds of the guests and carnival workers? Oops."

"Harley!" she could hear Batgirl saying. "When you destroyed his hat we got communication with the outside. Everything's back up and running."

"Hey, Batgirl," Harley said. "You got a dictionary? Can you look up something for me?"

"Sure," Batgirl said. "But, Harley, we're still trapped in the bubble, remember?"

"Not for long," Harley assured her.

"Hellloooooo, Harley Quinn here," Harley announced. Her face was on every screen at the Krazy Karnival, broadcasting to the world. "It's good to be back! I promised you a rematch of Harley's Battle of the Bands, and here we go."

Cheetah, Batgirl, and other Supers stopped trying to break the bubble with their powers and weapons, wondering what Harley was up to. "A music contest? Now?" Hawkgirl asked.

Miss Martian ran up to Harley. "I'm not sure this is the right time for a contest," she said.

Harley winked at her and said, "Read my mind."

Miss Martian shut her eyes, then nodded. "Oh, I see!" she said, not even hiding her delight.

"Battle of the Band contestants," Harley declared. "Start playing AS LOUD AS YOU CAN. And everyone—join in and MAKE SOME NOISE!"

The bands, who were scattered all over the amusement park, hurried to get themselves together. Instruments were plugged in and amplifiers were turned all the way up. Soon every band began to play. At first it sounded like a clash of wildly different styles and sounds at war with each other. But then something strange started to happen. The music began to mesh into a fusion no one had ever heard before.

The musical vibration began to make the bubble quiver.

"LOUDER!" Harley shouted. "I CAN'T HEAR YOU!"

"What's she doing?" Big Barda asked as she covered her ears.

Miss Martian closed her eyes and smiled. "She's breaking the bubble," she said.

Harley looked into her camera as the bubble began to shake, making its own deep trembling noise. "Harley Quinn here, live at the Krazy Karnival, where the Battle of the Bands is in session. But the musicians can't do it alone. To break the bubble we need to make a boisterous sound! More noise than you've ever heard before! It's gotta be LOUD! It's gotta be a sound so obstreperous—" She paused and said slowly to the camera, "That means noisy and difficult to control, according to the dictionary—that it cracks this bubble where it counts."

Supergirl and Wonder Woman began to fly around the amusement park to spread the news.

"Everyone make some noise!" Supergirl said.

"Louder!" Wonder Woman cried.

Bumblebee, Big Barda, Thunder, and Lightning began to sing. Beast Boy once more became a coqui frog and began to croak. Silver Banshee raised her sonic scream that was only matched by Captain Cold's wailing guitar solo.

Soon all the other Supers joined in, encouraging everyone to shout, sing, stomp, and bang anything to add to the ocean of sound started by the bands. With each voice and sound added, the bubble began to tremble more. But it still wouldn't break.

Miss Martian looked at Harley in desperation and cried out, "It's not enough. We need something more."

Everything that had happened lately raced through Harley's mind in fast-forward. Was she an Internet personality? A solid B student—okay, B-minus? A class clown? An entertainment impresario? And then she remembered who she was and a mischievous grin crossed her face.

I'm a **SUPER.**

Harley Quinn reached into her pocket and pulled out the strength-tester bell from earlier. Smiling, she tossed it into the air and then swung her mallet with all her might. *CLANG!* the iron bell rang out as it rocketed into the sky. It hit the vibrating bubble and smashed through it.

Everyone stopped making music and noise. For a moment, the absolute silence was as deafening as the cacophony.

"**YOWZA,**" Harley said quietly under her breath. And with that, the bubble **shattered!**

The bubble broke into a million shards and began to rain down on Krazy Karnival. Poison Ivy cried, "It's okay! It's safe! Look—rainbows!"

Sure enough, the big bubble that had once covered the Krazy Karnival turned into tiny rainbows that wafted downward and before they hit the ground.

"You're seeing it here in this Harley's Quinntessentials exclusive," Harley said, her signature smile broadcasting to her viewers. "The Mad Hatter is caught. The bubble is broken, the bad guys are rounded up, and the carnivalgoers are safe. And, wait, wait, I'm getting some news from Metropolis—" Via the jester hat, Harley listened as Batgirl plugged her in to Lois Lane. "Yes!" she went on. "I knew it! When the Mad Hatter's hat broke, so did the hold he had on the Green Team. They were under his control, but no more. In fact, they're apologizing and returning everything they took, right now. **WOWZA! YOWZA!** This is turning out A-okay, and . . ." Harley's smile froze on her face.

Principal Waller was marching toward her with all the Super Hero High teachers behind her.

CHAPTER 30

"We cut our conference short when danger arose, but we couldn't get past the bubble," Principal Waller said. Liberty Belle, Mr. Fox, Wildcat, and the other teachers nodded. Parasite, the janitor, looked around at the mess that was the Krazy Karnival and sighed.

Harley shrugged. "Um, I'm in trouble again, right?" she asked. "Hiya, VP Grodd, guess I'll see you in detention tomorrow!"

"Quite the contrary," Waller informed her. "What is happening is highly unorthodox—but then, so are you. Harley Quinn," Principal Waller continued in a booming voice, "it is my honor to name you Super Hero High's Super Hero of the Month!"

For once Harley was speechless—but not for long. "**WOWZA!**" she yelled as cheers erupted. "ME?!"

"YOU!" Pied Piper called out. He turned to the bands and gave them the signal to start playing.

When Waller handed Harley the official Hero of the Month award, Harley hugged it and then backflipped onto the top of a tall Sweet Treats stand. Harley looked out over all the Supers who had gathered around. With a mischievous glint in her eyes, Harley threw her award high into the air.

"This award doesn't belong to me. It belongs to all of us. Yes, I'm lookin' at you!" she said when Miss Martian caught it. Harley pointed. "And you, and you, and you, and you! I declare EVERYONE the winners of the Battle of the Bands, and the Battle Against Mad Hatter, and the Breakers of the Bubble! We are all winners here!"

Cheetah looked up at Harley. "Is there a class clown award?"

Harley winced. Waller had just named her a hero and now Cheetah was bringing up the class clown thing again?

But when Cheetah turned to the crowd, Harley could hardly believe what she was hearing. "Hat's off to Harley Quinn, Super Hero High's very own one-of-a-kind class clown," Cheetah said. Breaking into a grin, Cheetah started to shout, "Harley! Harley!"

Harley's heart swelled as the crowd began to chant "HARLEY! HARLEY! HARLEY!"

As the chant grew to a thunderous roar, Harley dove off the top of the Sweet Treats stand, and hundreds of hands rose to catch her.

As Lois interviewed Harley on camera in front of Capes & Cowls Café, Miss Martian stood off to the side, watching. She clutched a basket overflowing with fan letters from people who had been inside the bubble and outside who had learned of her bravery. While Harley chatted effortlessly, Miss Martian was trying not to disappear, since her interview was up next.

Thunder and Lightning waved to Harley as they raced inside. Beast Boy, as a baby kangaroo, kept jumping up and down, photobombing the interview. Bumblebee's phone rang with its familiar "Flight of the Bumblebee" ringtone. But Harley, ever the pro, stayed focused.

"The safety of the world was more important than how many people were watching my show," she was saying. "Mad Hatter wanted the audience, but I wanted to save the world from him."

"You heard it here," Lois said to the camera. "It's no joke

that Harley Quinn is a real hero. So what's next for Harley's Quinntessentials?"

"Well, now that the Green Team is taking over the Krazy Karnival and donating any profits to charity, I'll be covering that. Plus, I plan to start a new segment called 'Good Deed of the Day,' featuring Supers and citizens helping others. . . .'"

Bumblebee started gasping for air as Harley was talking. Supergirl and Poison Ivy rushed to her. Lois cut off the interview. "Are you okay?" she asked.

By then Bumblebee was in tears.

"Bumblebee?" said Harley.

Bumblebee put down her phone. "My mom and dad are in danger!" she cried. "I have to go!" She turned herself small and rushed to fly away before anyone could stop her.

Poison Ivy shouted after her. "Bumblebee, what's happening?"

But Bumblebee couldn't hear her. By then she was already past Metropolis.

To be continued . . .

Mieke Kramer

After writing jingles, restaurant menus, and TV shows, Lisa Yee won the prestigious Sid Fleischman Humor Award for her debut novel, *Millicent Min, Girl Genius*. Her other novels for young readers include *Stanford Wong Flunks Big-Time*, *Bobby vs. Girls (Accidentally)*, and several books for American Girl, plus *Warp Speed*, about a Star Trek geek. Her most recent original YA novel is *The Kidney Hypothetical*. She has also written for *Huffington Post* and is a contributor to NPR.

Lisa's books have been named a *Washington Post* Book of the Week, a *USA Today* Critics' Pick, an NPR Best Summer Read, and more. Writing the DC Super Hero Girls series is a dream come true, says Lisa. "I get to hang out with Wonder Woman, Batgirl, Katana, and the rest of the super heroes!"

You can visit Lisa Yee at LisaYee.com.

SUPER HERO HIGH ISN'T LIKE MOST HIGH SCHOOLS

Fly High with All of the DC Super Hero Girls

WONDER WOMAN at **SUPER HERO HIGH**
BY LISA YEE

SUPERGIRL at **SUPER HERO HIGH**
BY LISA YEE

BATGIRL at **SUPER HERO HIGH**
BY LISA YEE

KATANA at **SUPER HERO HIGH**
BY LISA YEE

DCSuperHeroGirls.com